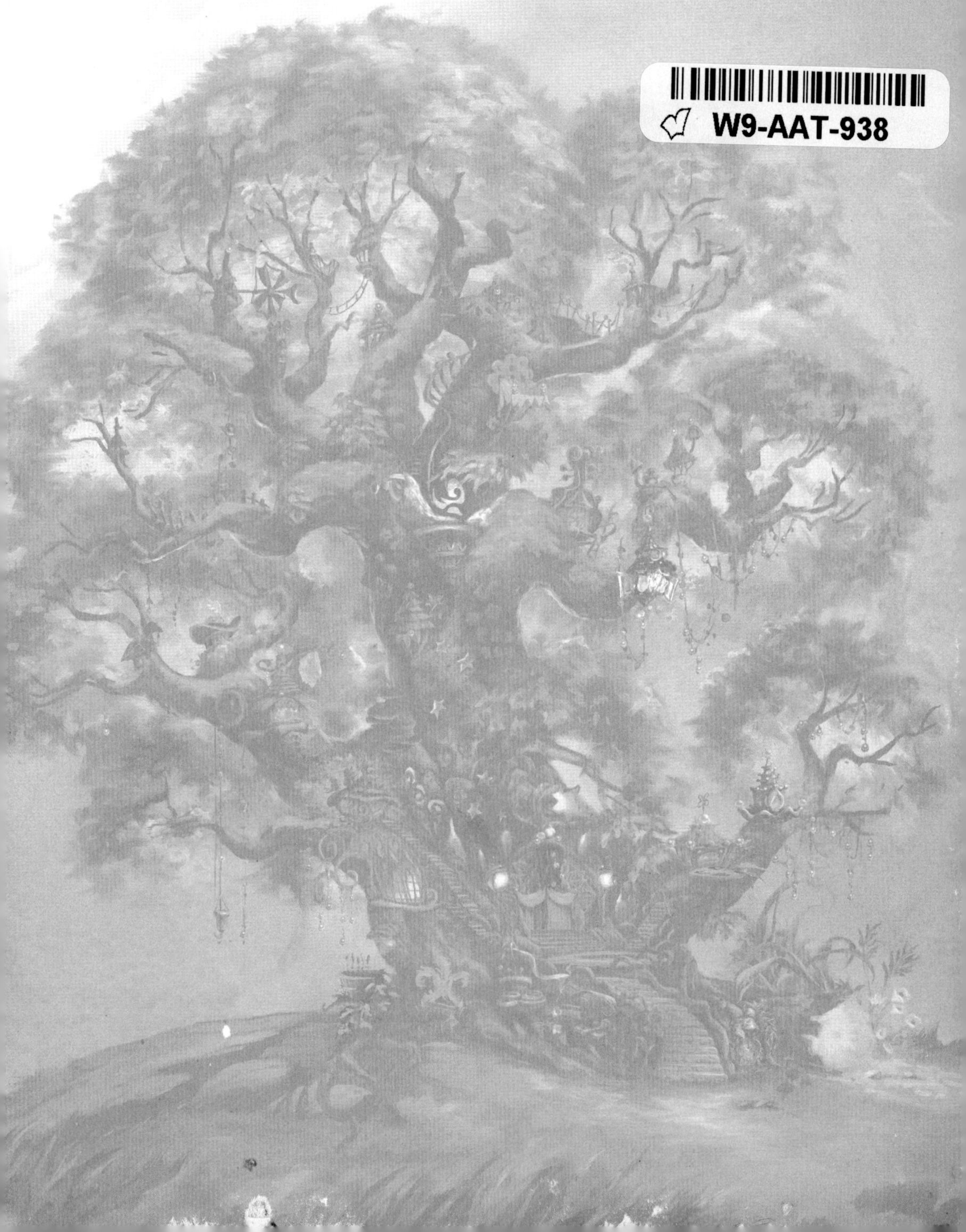

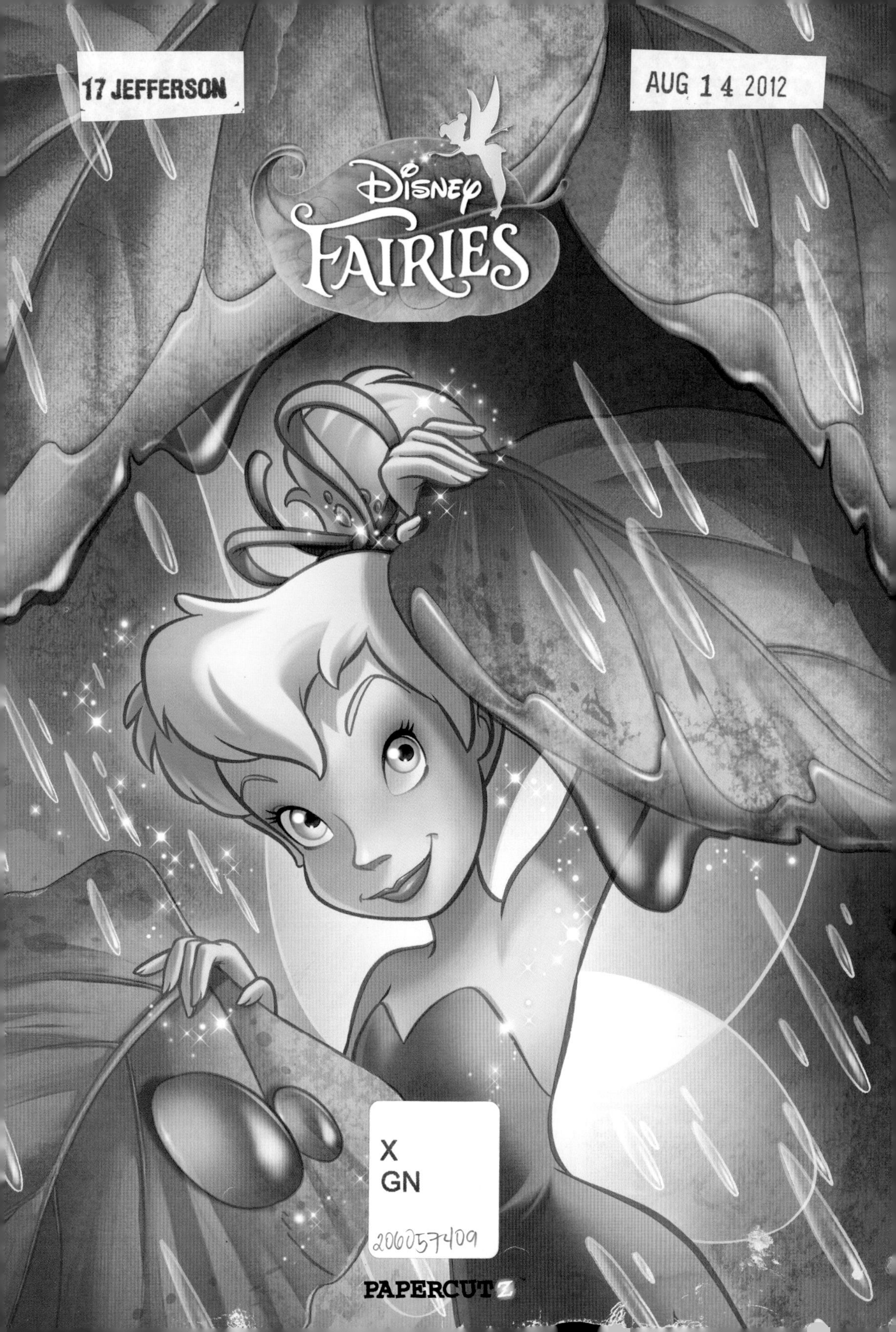
Disney
FAIRIES
PAPERCUTZ

Disney FAIRIES

Graphic Novels Available from
PAPERCUTZ

Graphic Novel #1

"Prilla's Talent"

Graphic Novel #2

"Tinker Bell and the
Wings of Rani"

Graphic Novel #3

"Tinker Bell and the Day
of the Dragon"

Graphic Novel #4

"Tinker Bell to the Rescue"

Graphic Novel #5

"Tinker Bell and
the Pirate Adventure"

Graphic Novel #6

"A Present for Tinker Bell"

Graphic Novel #7

"Tinker Bell the
Perfect Fairy"

Graphic Novel #8

"Tinker Bell and her Stories
for a Rainy Day"

**Tinker Bell and
the Great Fairy Rescue**

Coming Soon:

Graphic Novel #9

"Tinker Bell and her Magical Arrival"

#8 "Tinker Bell and her Stories for a Rainy Day"

Contents

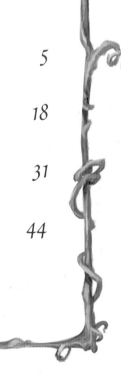

PAPERCUTZ™

NEW YORK

"Impossible Portraits"
Script: Augusto Macchetto
Revised Dialogue: Cortney Faye Powell
Pencils: Augusto Macchetto
Inks: Cristina Giorgilli
Color: Stefania Santi
Letters: Janice Chiang
Page 5 Art:
Pencils: Gianluca Barone
Inks: Marina Baggio
Color: Andrea Cagol

"Dulcie's Secret Ingredients""
Script: Paola Mulazzi
Revised Dialogue: Cortney Faye Powell
Pencils: Elisabetta Melaranci
Inks: Marina Baggio
Color: Stefania Santi
Letters: Janice Chiang
Page 18 Art:
Pencils: Caterina Giorgetti
Inks: Roberta Zanotta
Color: Andrea Cagol

"Butterfly Wings"
Script: Silvia Gianatti
Revised Dialogue: Cortney Faye Powell
Pencils: Emilio Urbano and Manuela Razzi
Inks: Roberta Zanotta
Color: Stefania Santi
Letters: Janice Chiang
Page 31 Art:
Pencils: Gianluca Barone
Inks: Marina Baggio
Color: Andrea Cagol

"Tinker Bell and her Stories For a Rainy Day"
Script: Augusto Macchetto
Revised Dialogue: Cortney Faye Powell
Pencils: Elisabetta Mclaranci
Inks: Cristina Giorgilli
Color: Stefania Santi
Letters: Janice Chiang
Page 44 Art:
Pencils: Caterina Giorgetti
Inks: Marina Baggio
Color: Andrea Cagol

Preview of "A Fairy Might Be Near"
Script: Augusto Maccetto
Revised Dialogue: Cortney Faye Powell
Pencils and Inks: Antonello Dalena
Color: Kawaii Creative Studio
Lettering: Janice Chiang

Nelson Design Group – Production
Special Thanks – Jesse Post and Shiho Tilley
Michael Petranek – Associate Editor
Jim Salicrup
Editor-in-Chief

ISBN: 978-1-59707-303-5 paperback edition
ISBN: 978-1-59707-304-2 hardcover edition

Printed in Singapore. October 2012
by Tien Wah Press PTE LTD
4 Pandan Crescent
Singapore 128475

Distributed by Macmillan

First Papercutz Printing

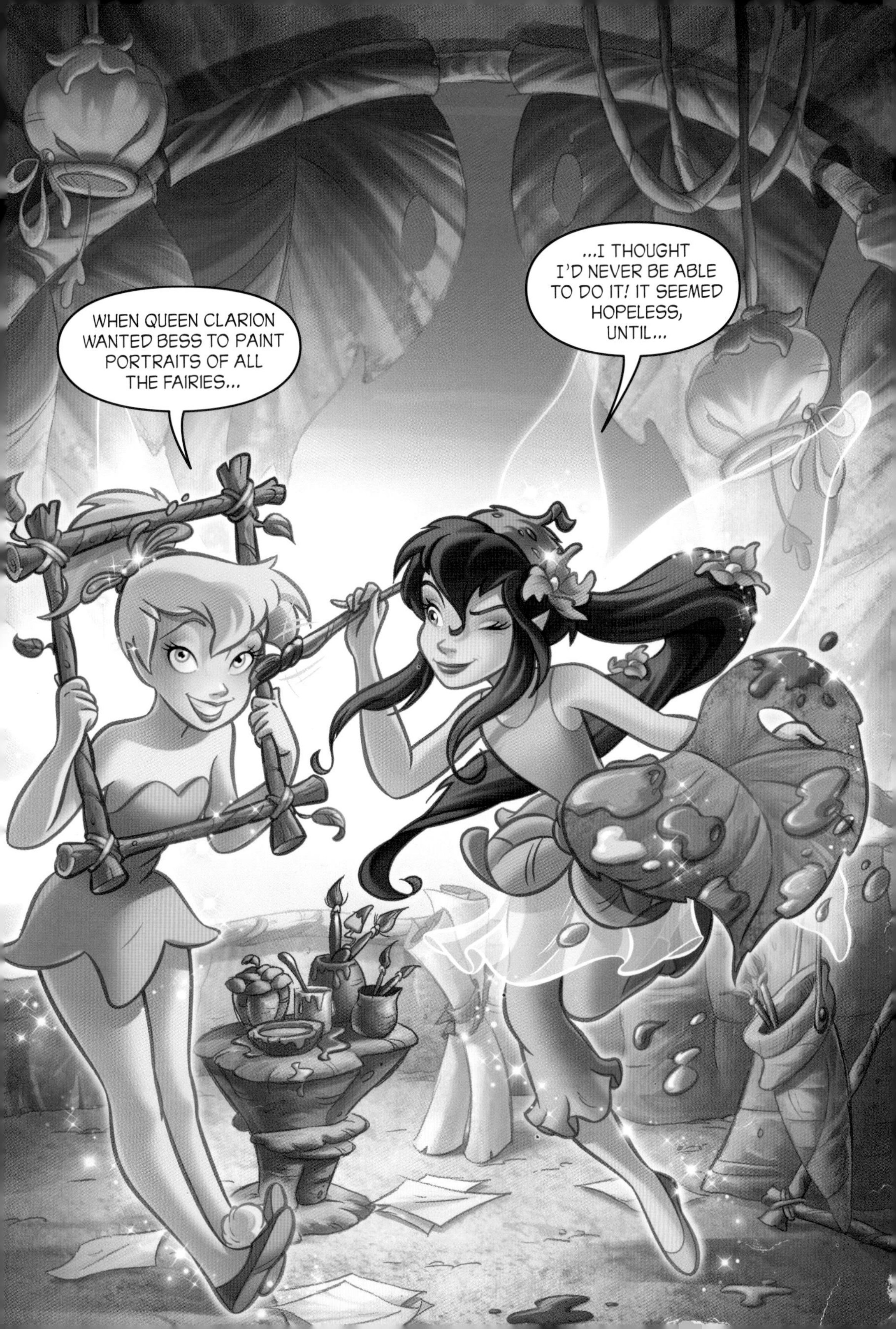
WHEN QUEEN CLARION WANTED BESS TO PAINT PORTRAITS OF ALL THE FAIRIES...
...I THOUGHT I'D NEVER BE ABLE TO DO IT! IT SEEMED HOPELESS, UNTIL...

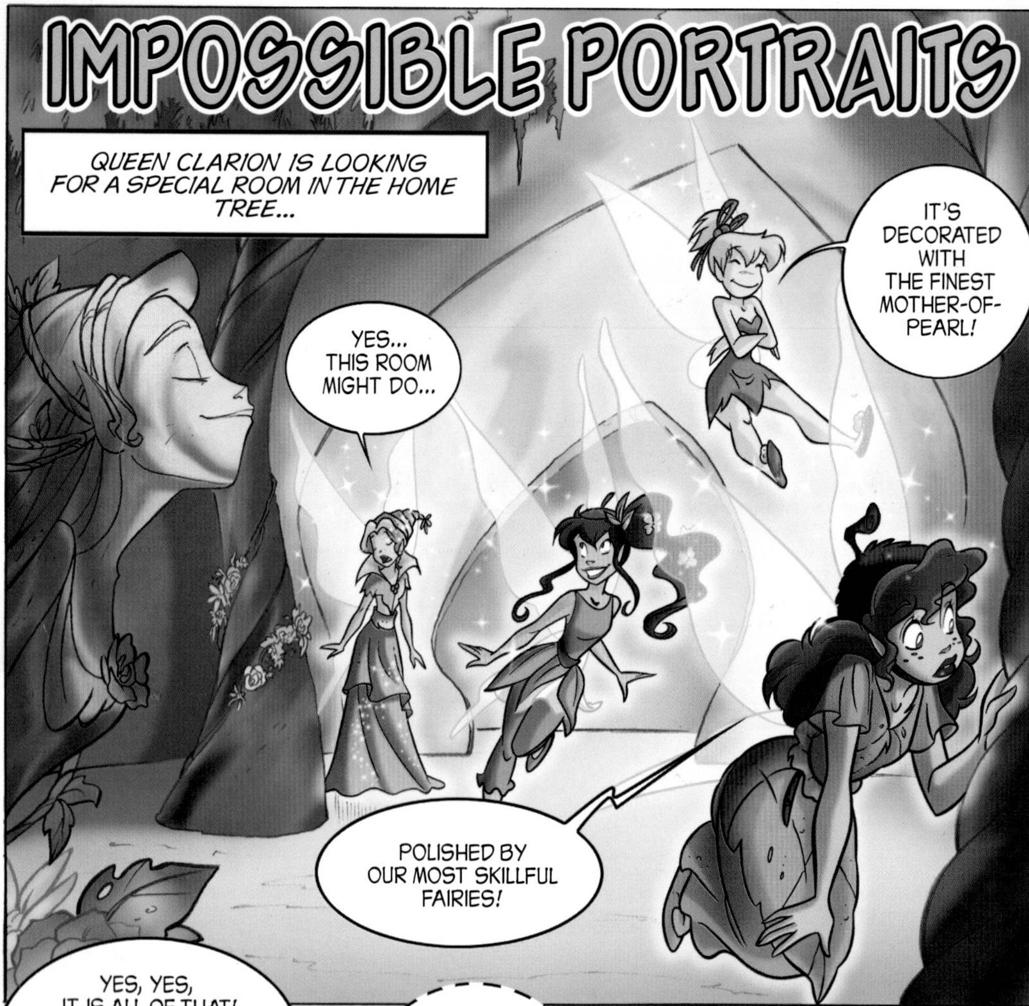
IMPOSSIBLE PORTRAITS
QUEEN CLARION IS LOOKING FOR A SPECIAL ROOM IN THE HOME TREE...
YES... THIS ROOM MIGHT DO...
IT'S DECORATED WITH THE FINEST MOTHER-OF-PEARL!
POLISHED BY OUR MOST SKILLFUL FAIRIES!

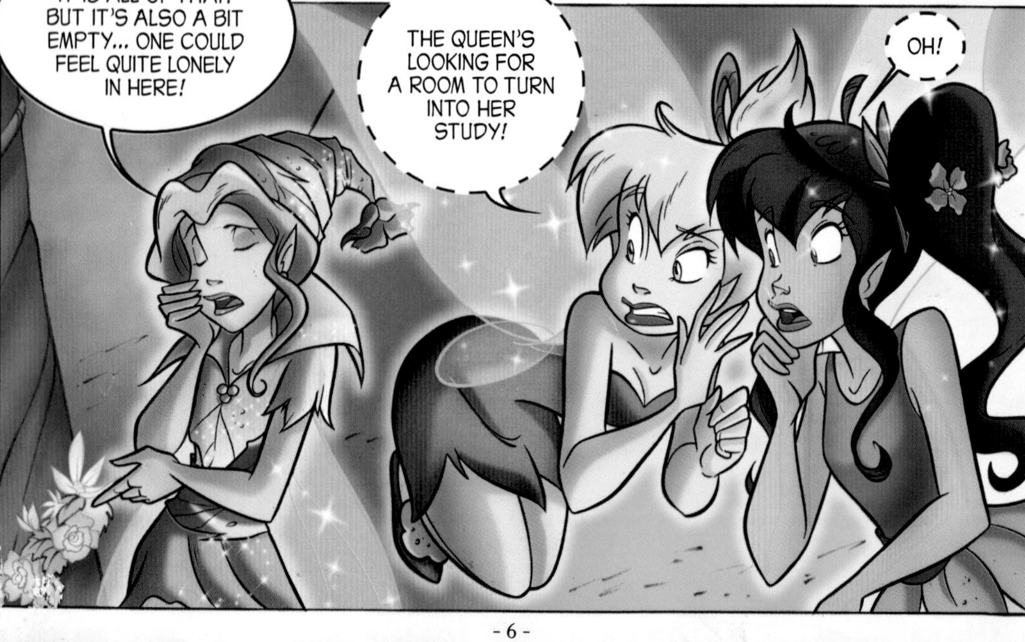
YES, YES, IT IS ALL OF THAT! BUT IT'S ALSO A BIT EMPTY... ONE COULD FEEL QUITE LONELY IN HERE!
THE QUEEN'S LOOKING FOR A ROOM TO TURN INTO HER STUDY!
OH!

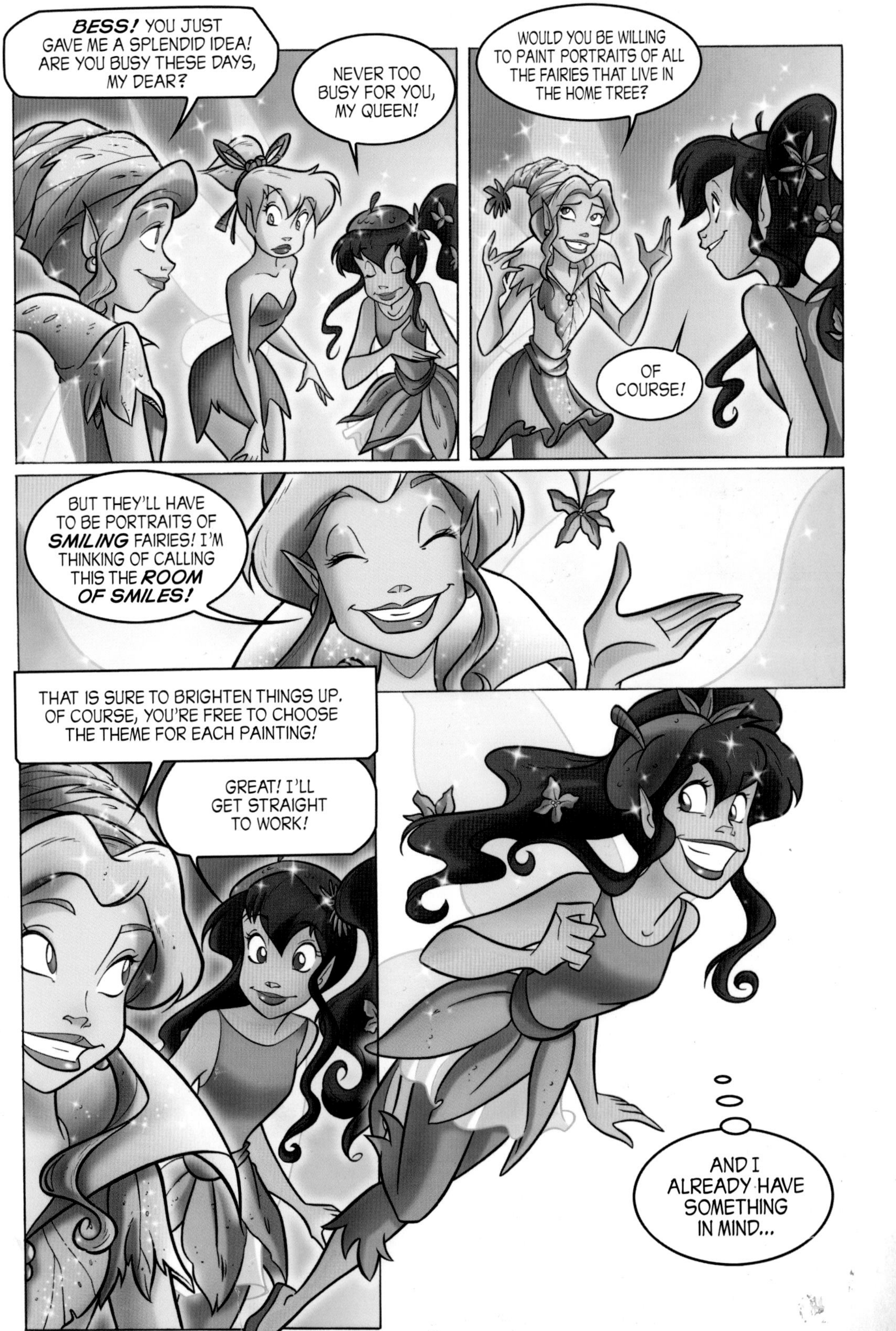
BESS! YOU JUST GAVE ME A SPLENDID IDEA! ARE YOU BUSY THESE DAYS, MY DEAR?
NEVER TOO BUSY FOR YOU, MY QUEEN!
WOULD YOU BE WILLING TO PAINT PORTRAITS OF ALL THE FAIRIES THAT LIVE IN THE HOME TREE?
OF COURSE!
BUT THEY'LL HAVE TO BE PORTRAITS OF **SMILING** FAIRIES! I'M THINKING OF CALLING THIS THE **ROOM OF SMILES!**
THAT IS SURE TO BRIGHTEN THINGS UP. OF COURSE, YOU'RE FREE TO CHOOSE THE THEME FOR EACH PAINTING!
GREAT! I'LL GET STRAIGHT TO WORK!
AND I ALREADY HAVE SOMETHING IN MIND...

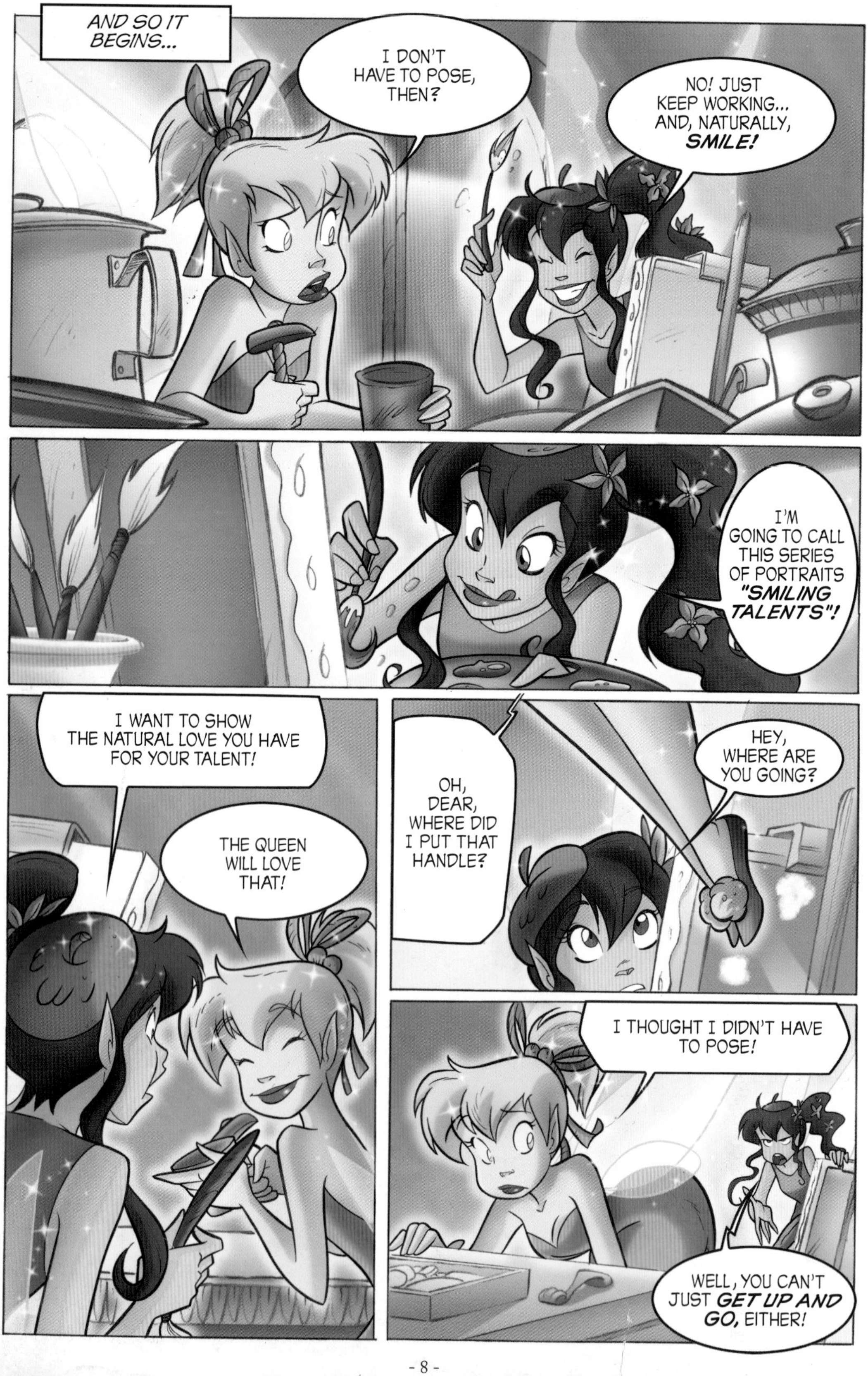
AND SO IT BEGINS...
I DON'T HAVE TO POSE, THEN?
NO! JUST KEEP WORKING... AND, NATURALLY, SMILE!
I'M GOING TO CALL THIS SERIES OF PORTRAITS "SMILING TALENTS"!
I WANT TO SHOW THE NATURAL LOVE YOU HAVE FOR YOUR TALENT!
THE QUEEN WILL LOVE THAT!
OH, DEAR, WHERE DID I PUT THAT HANDLE?
HEY, WHERE ARE YOU GOING?
I THOUGHT I DIDN'T HAVE TO POSE!
WELL, YOU CAN'T JUST GET UP AND GO, EITHER!

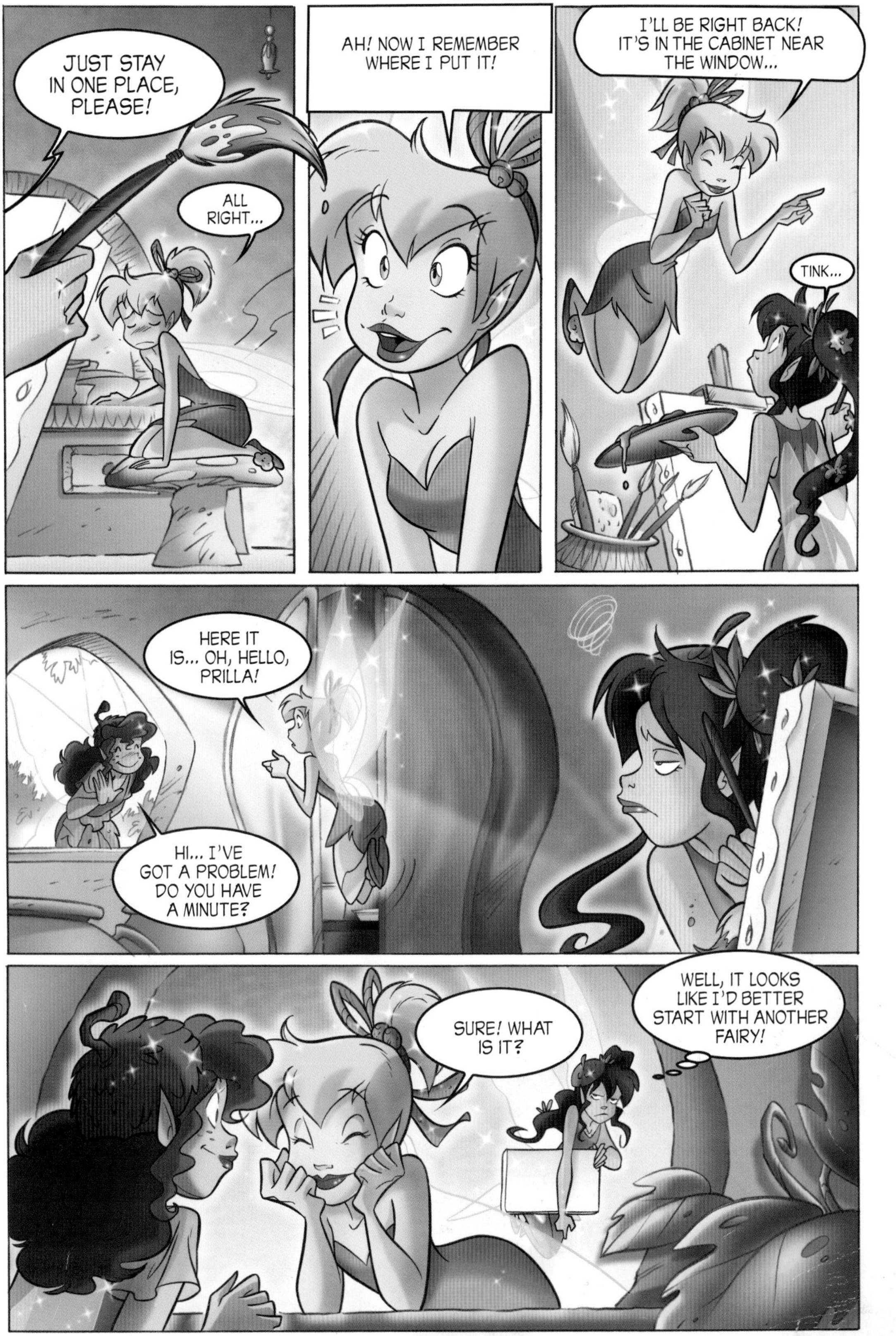
JUST STAY IN ONE PLACE, PLEASE!
ALL RIGHT...
AH! NOW I REMEMBER WHERE I PUT IT!
I'LL BE RIGHT BACK! IT'S IN THE CABINET NEAR THE WINDOW...
TINK...
HERE IT IS... OH, HELLO, PRILLA!
HI... I'VE GOT A PROBLEM! DO YOU HAVE A MINUTE?
SURE! WHAT IS IT?
WELL, IT LOOKS LIKE I'D BETTER START WITH ANOTHER FAIRY!

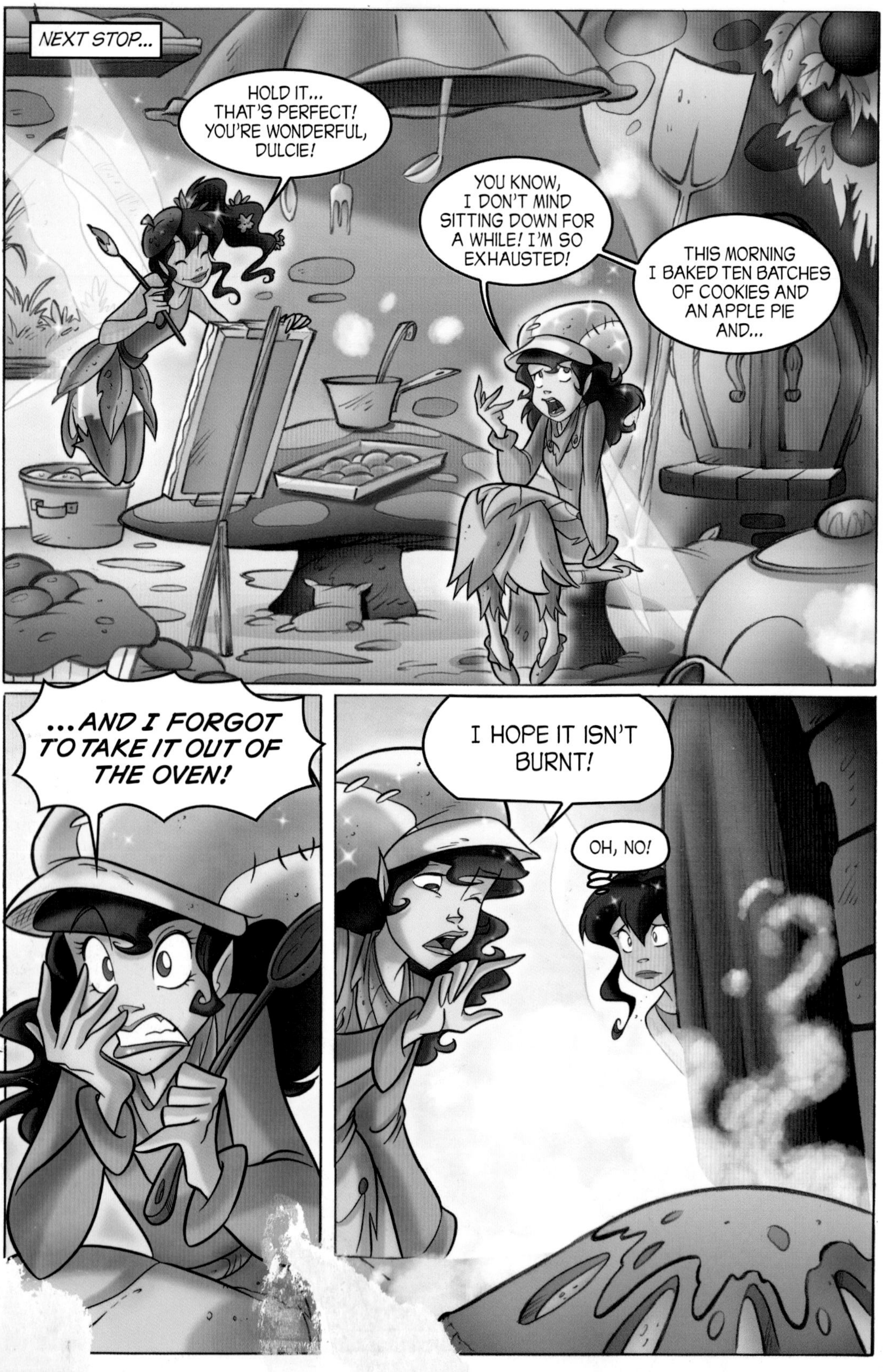
NEXT STOP...
HOLD IT... THAT'S PERFECT! YOU'RE WONDERFUL, DULCIE!
YOU KNOW, I DON'T MIND SITTING DOWN FOR A WHILE! I'M SO EXHAUSTED!
THIS MORNING I BAKED TEN BATCHES OF COOKIES AND AN APPLE PIE AND...
...AND I FORGOT TO TAKE IT OUT OF THE OVEN!
I HOPE IT ISN'T BURNT!
OH, NO!

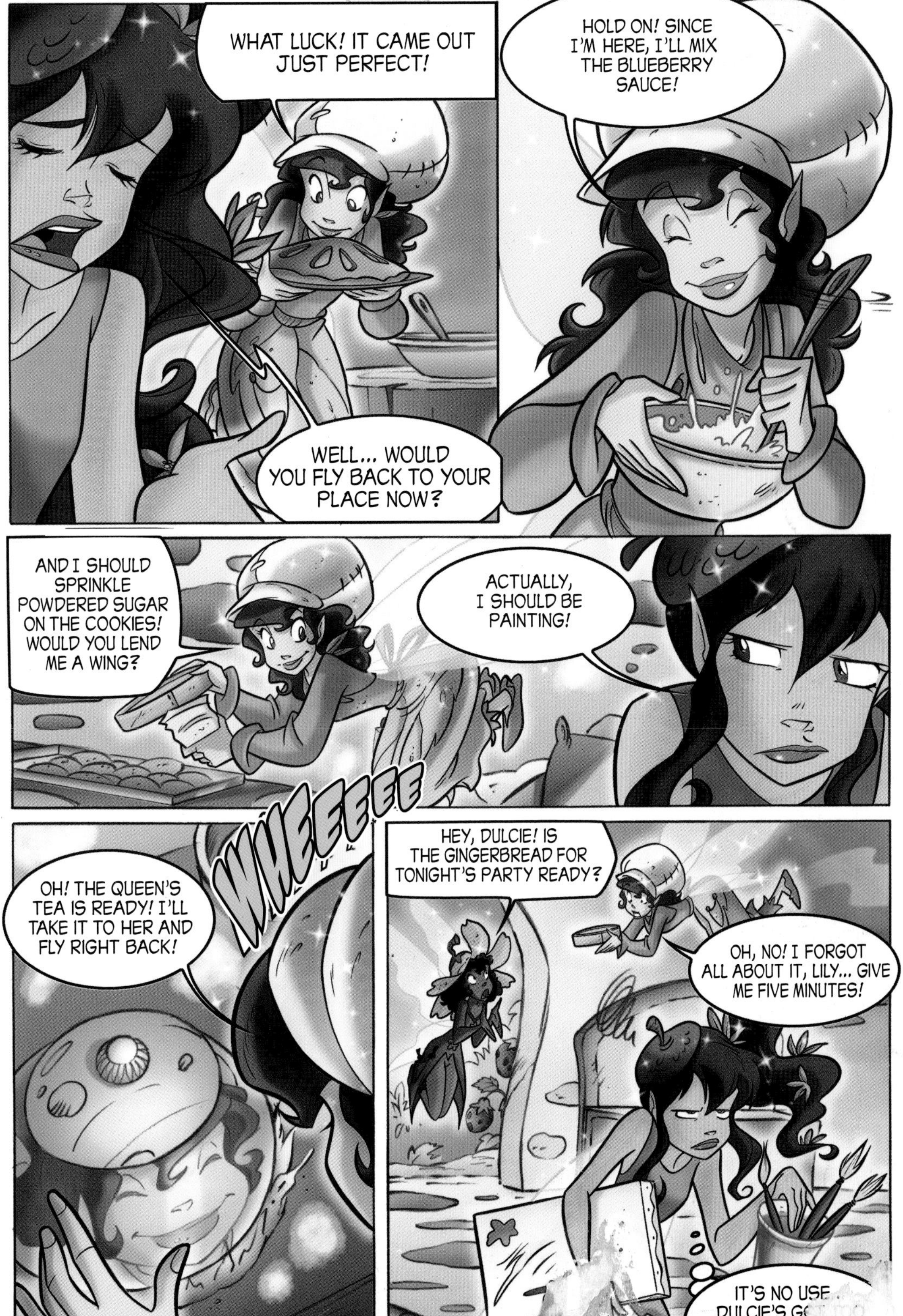
WHAT LUCK! IT CAME OUT JUST PERFECT!
WELL... WOULD YOU FLY BACK TO YOUR PLACE NOW?
HOLD ON! SINCE I'M HERE, I'LL MIX THE BLUEBERRY SAUCE!
AND I SHOULD SPRINKLE POWDERED SUGAR ON THE COOKIES! WOULD YOU LEND ME A WING?
ACTUALLY, I SHOULD BE PAINTING!
WHEEEEE
OH! THE QUEEN'S TEA IS READY! I'LL TAKE IT TO HER AND FLY RIGHT BACK!
HEY, DULCIE! IS THE GINGERBREAD FOR TONIGHT'S PARTY READY?
OH, NO! I FORGOT ALL ABOUT IT, LILY... GIVE ME FIVE MINUTES!
IT'S NO USE
DULCIE'S G
MUCH ON HE
TO PO

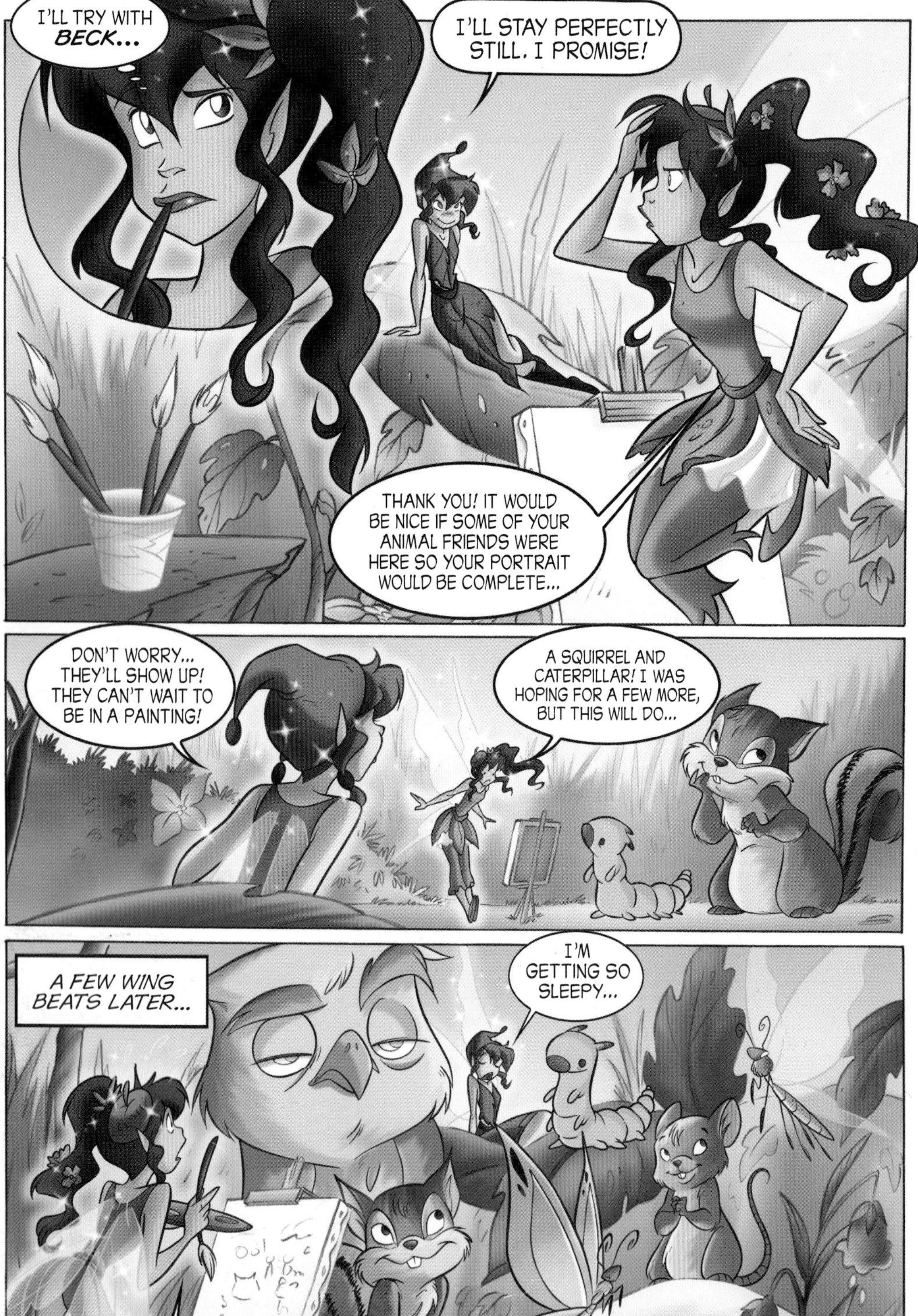

I'LL TRY WITH BECK...
I'LL STAY PERFECTLY STILL. I PROMISE!
THANK YOU! IT WOULD BE NICE IF SOME OF YOUR ANIMAL FRIENDS WERE HERE SO YOUR PORTRAIT WOULD BE COMPLETE...
DON'T WORRY... THEY'LL SHOW UP! THEY CAN'T WAIT TO BE IN A PAINTING!
A SQUIRREL AND CATERPILLAR! I WAS HOPING FOR A FEW MORE, BUT THIS WILL DO...
A FEW WING BEATS LATER...
I'M GETTING SO SLEEPY...
SIGH! A BIT MUCH, BUT I CAN MANAGE, AS LONG AS I GET A CLEAR VIEW OF BECK...

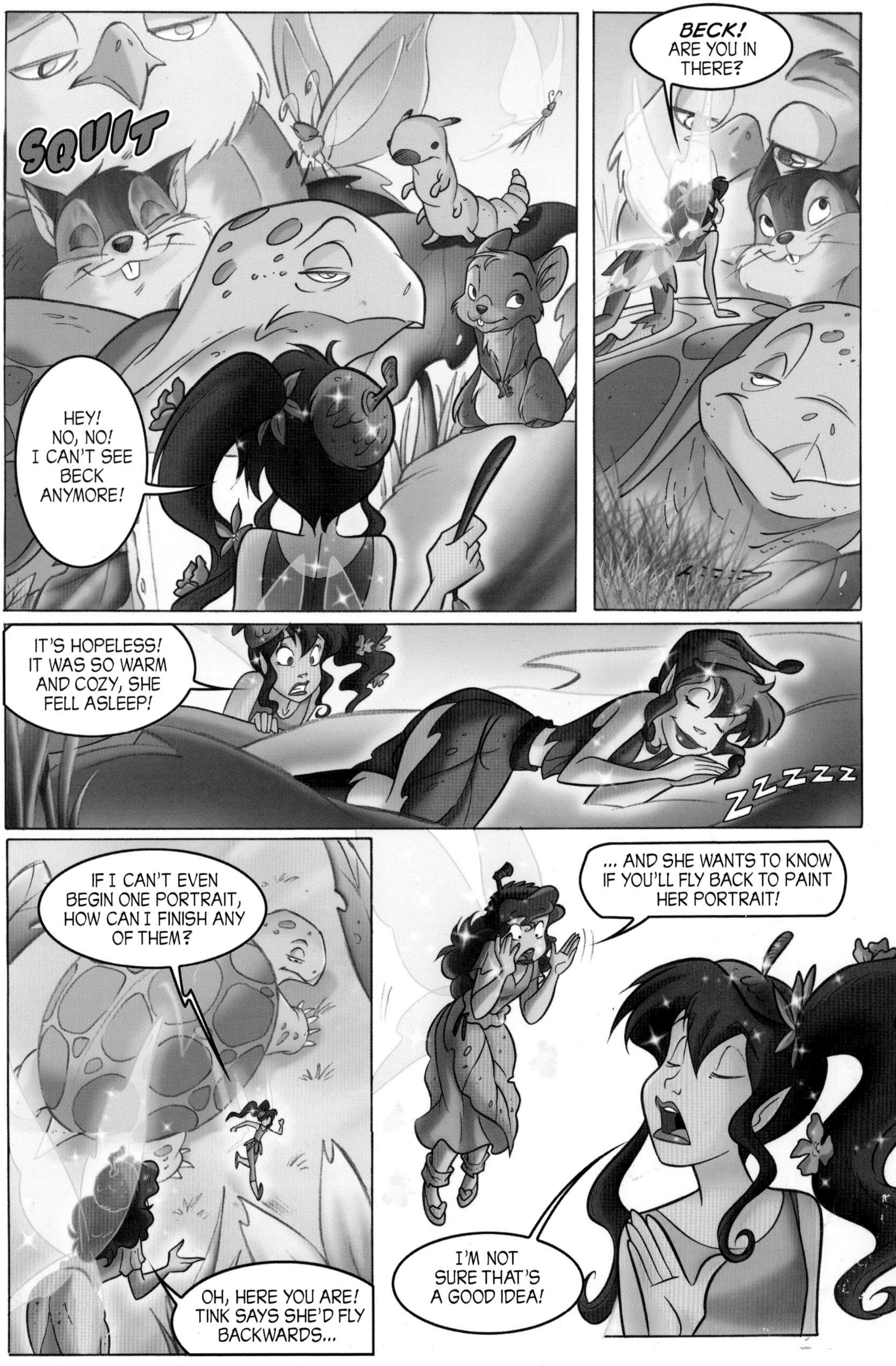
SQUIT
HEY! NO, NO! I CAN'T SEE BECK ANYMORE!
BECK! ARE YOU IN THERE?
IT'S HOPELESS! IT WAS SO WARM AND COZY, SHE FELL ASLEEP!
ZZZZZ
IF I CAN'T EVEN BEGIN ONE PORTRAIT, HOW CAN I FINISH ANY OF THEM?
OH, HERE YOU ARE! TINK SAYS SHE'D FLY BACKWARDS...
... AND SHE WANTS TO KNOW IF YOU'LL FLY BACK TO PAINT HER PORTRAIT!
I'M NOT SURE THAT'S A GOOD IDEA!

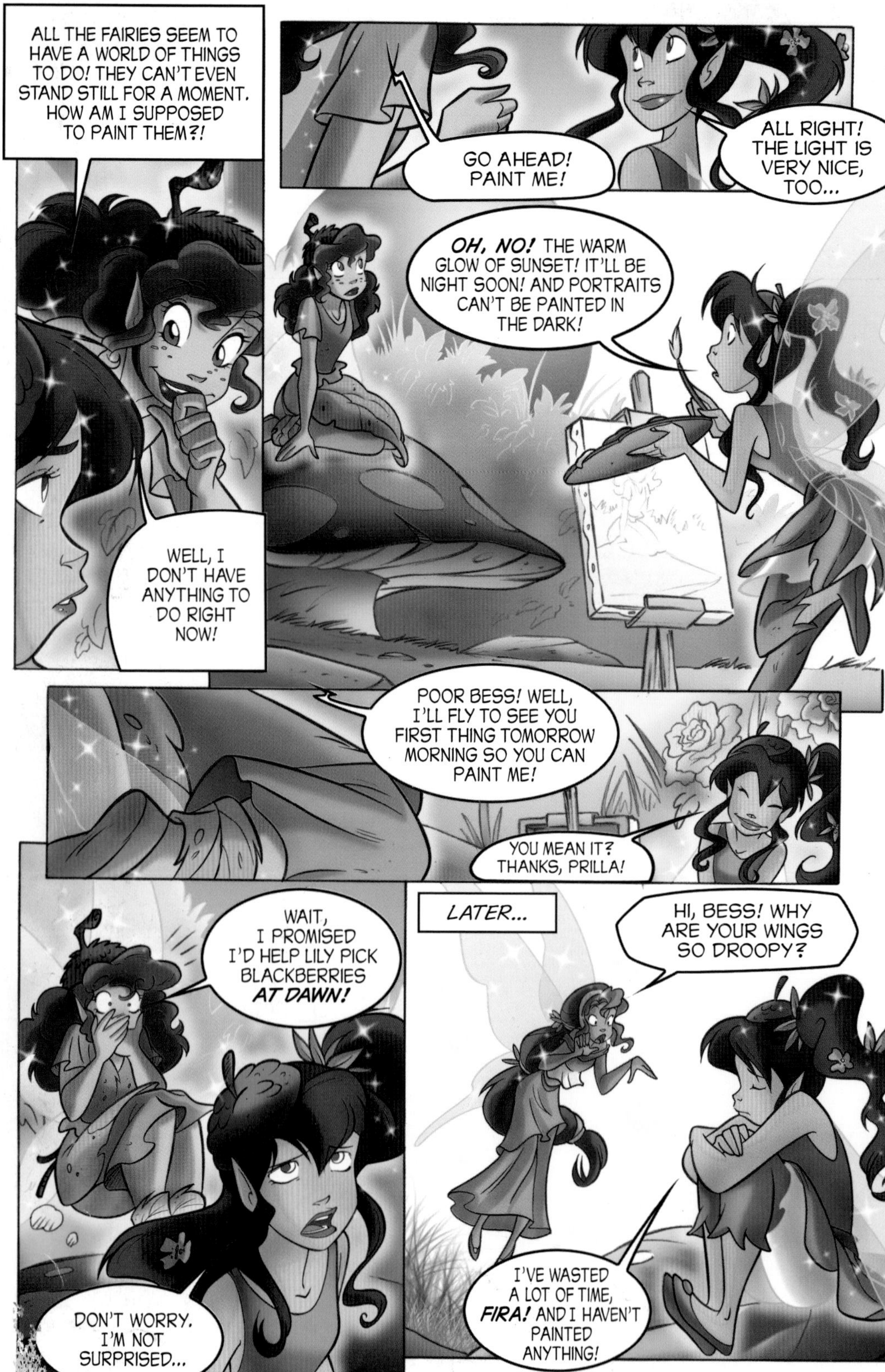

ALL THE FAIRIES SEEM TO HAVE A WORLD OF THINGS TO DO! THEY CAN'T EVEN STAND STILL FOR A MOMENT. HOW AM I SUPPOSED TO PAINT THEM?!
WELL, I DON'T HAVE ANYTHING TO DO RIGHT NOW!
GO AHEAD! PAINT ME!
ALL RIGHT! THE LIGHT IS VERY NICE, TOO...
OH, NO! THE WARM GLOW OF SUNSET! IT'LL BE NIGHT SOON! AND PORTRAITS CAN'T BE PAINTED IN THE DARK!
POOR BESS! WELL, I'LL FLY TO SEE YOU FIRST THING TOMORROW MORNING SO YOU CAN PAINT ME!
YOU MEAN IT? THANKS, PRILLA!
WAIT, I PROMISED I'D HELP LILY PICK BLACKBERRIES AT DAWN!
DON'T WORRY. I'M NOT SURPRISED...
LATER...
HI, BESS! WHY ARE YOUR WINGS SO DROOPY?
I'VE WASTED A LOT OF TIME, FIRA! AND I HAVEN'T PAINTED ANYTHING!

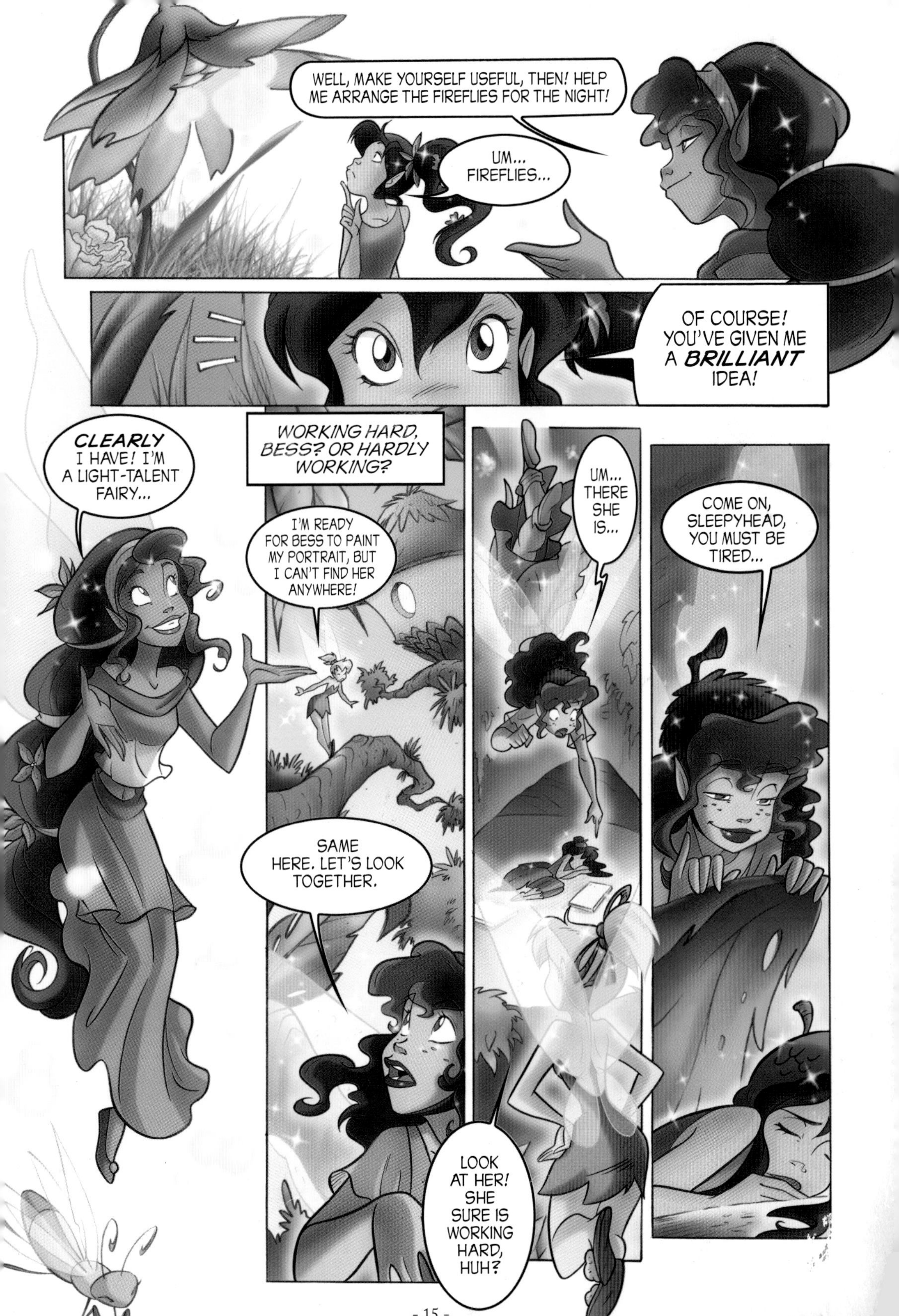
WELL, MAKE YOURSELF USEFUL, THEN! HELP ME ARRANGE THE FIREFLIES FOR THE NIGHT!
UM... FIREFLIES...
OF COURSE! YOU'VE GIVEN ME A BRILLIANT IDEA!
CLEARLY I HAVE! I'M A LIGHT-TALENT FAIRY...
WORKING HARD, BESS? OR HARDLY WORKING?
I'M READY FOR BESS TO PAINT MY PORTRAIT, BUT I CAN'T FIND HER ANYWHERE!
SAME HERE. LET'S LOOK TOGETHER.
UM... THERE SHE IS...
LOOK AT HER! SHE SURE IS WORKING HARD, HUH?
COME ON, SLEEPYHEAD, YOU MUST BE TIRED...

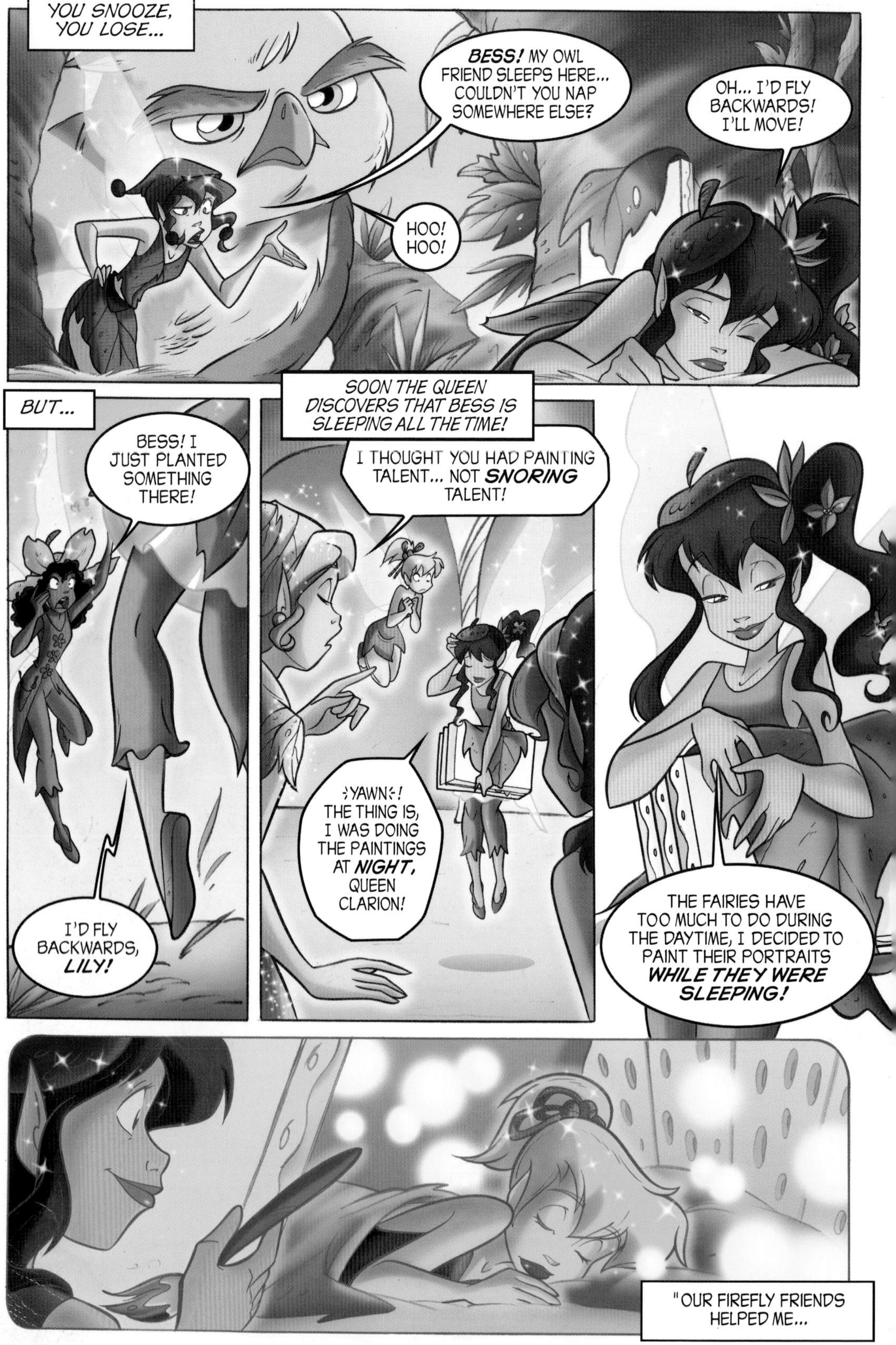
YOU SNOOZE, YOU LOSE...
BESS! MY OWL FRIEND SLEEPS HERE... COULDN'T YOU NAP SOMEWHERE ELSE?
HOO! HOO!
OH... I'D FLY BACKWARDS! I'LL MOVE!
BUT...
BESS! I JUST PLANTED SOMETHING THERE!
I'D FLY BACKWARDS, LILY!
SOON THE QUEEN DISCOVERS THAT BESS IS SLEEPING ALL THE TIME!
I THOUGHT YOU HAD PAINTING TALENT... NOT SNORING TALENT!
YAWN! THE THING IS, I WAS DOING THE PAINTINGS AT NIGHT, QUEEN CLARION!
THE FAIRIES HAVE TOO MUCH TO DO DURING THE DAYTIME, I DECIDED TO PAINT THEIR PORTRAITS WHILE THEY WERE SLEEPING!
"OUR FIREFLY FRIENDS HELPED ME...

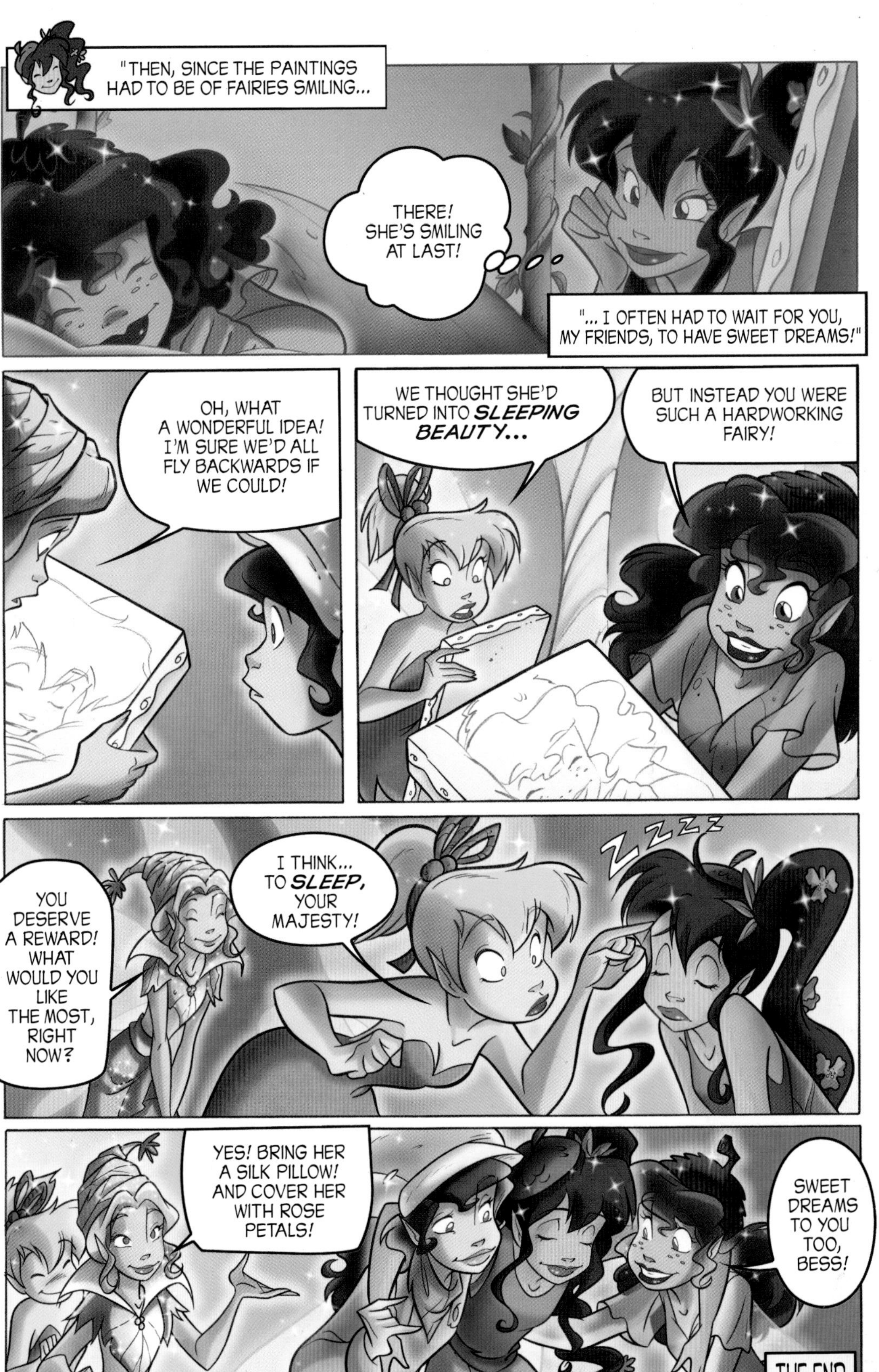
"THEN, SINCE THE PAINTINGS HAD TO BE OF FAIRIES SMILING...
THERE! SHE'S SMILING AT LAST!
"... I OFTEN HAD TO WAIT FOR YOU, MY FRIENDS, TO HAVE SWEET DREAMS!"
OH, WHAT A WONDERFUL IDEA! I'M SURE WE'D ALL FLY BACKWARDS IF WE COULD!
WE THOUGHT SHE'D TURNED INTO SLEEPING BEAUTY...
BUT INSTEAD YOU WERE SUCH A HARDWORKING FAIRY!
YOU DESERVE A REWARD! WHAT WOULD YOU LIKE THE MOST, RIGHT NOW?
I THINK... TO SLEEP, YOUR MAJESTY!
ZZZZ
YES! BRING HER A SILK PILLOW! AND COVER HER WITH ROSE PETALS!
SWEET DREAMS TO YOU TOO, BESS!
THE END

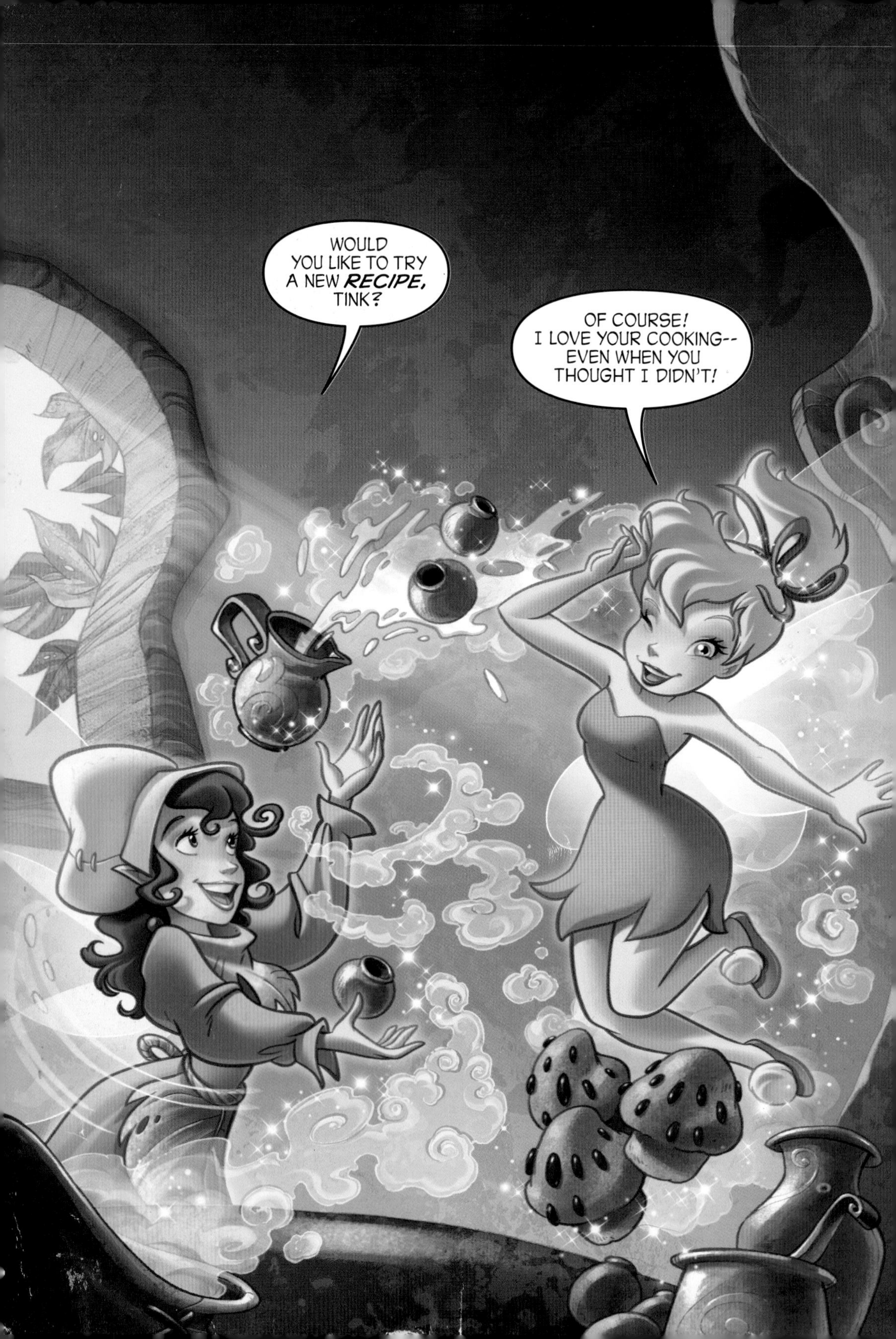
WOULD YOU LIKE TO TRY A NEW RECIPE, TINK?
OF COURSE! I LOVE YOUR COOKING-- EVEN WHEN YOU THOUGHT I DIDN'T!

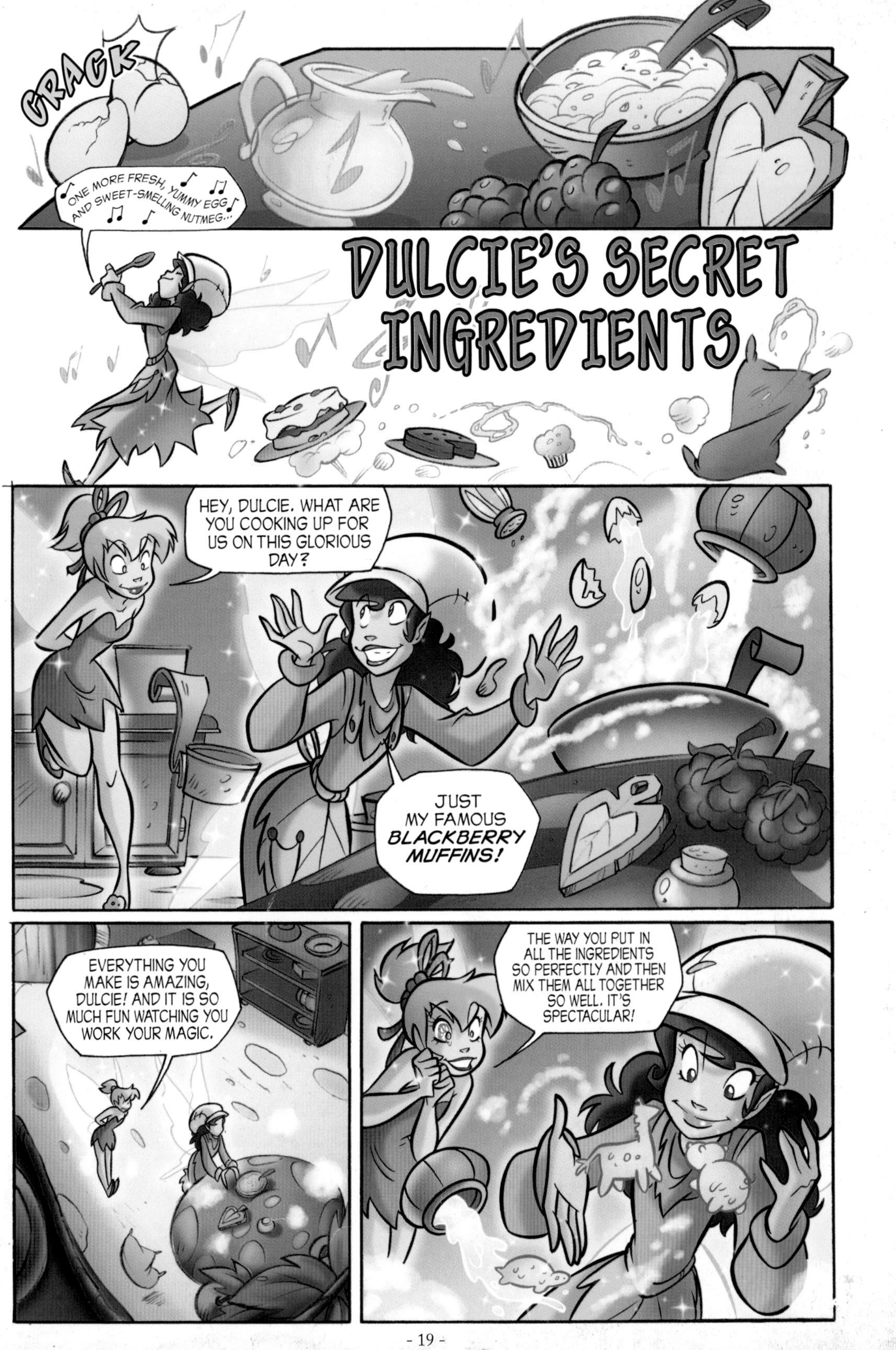
CRACK
ONE MORE FRESH, YUMMY EGG AND SWEET-SMELLING NUTMEG...
DULCIE'S SECRET INGREDIENTS
HEY, DULCIE. WHAT ARE YOU COOKING UP FOR US ON THIS GLORIOUS DAY?
JUST MY FAMOUS BLACKBERRY MUFFINS!
EVERYTHING YOU MAKE IS AMAZING, DULCIE! AND IT IS SO MUCH FUN WATCHING YOU WORK YOUR MAGIC.
THE WAY YOU PUT IN ALL THE INGREDIENTS SO PERFECTLY AND THEN MIX THEM ALL TOGETHER SO WELL. IT'S SPECTACULAR!

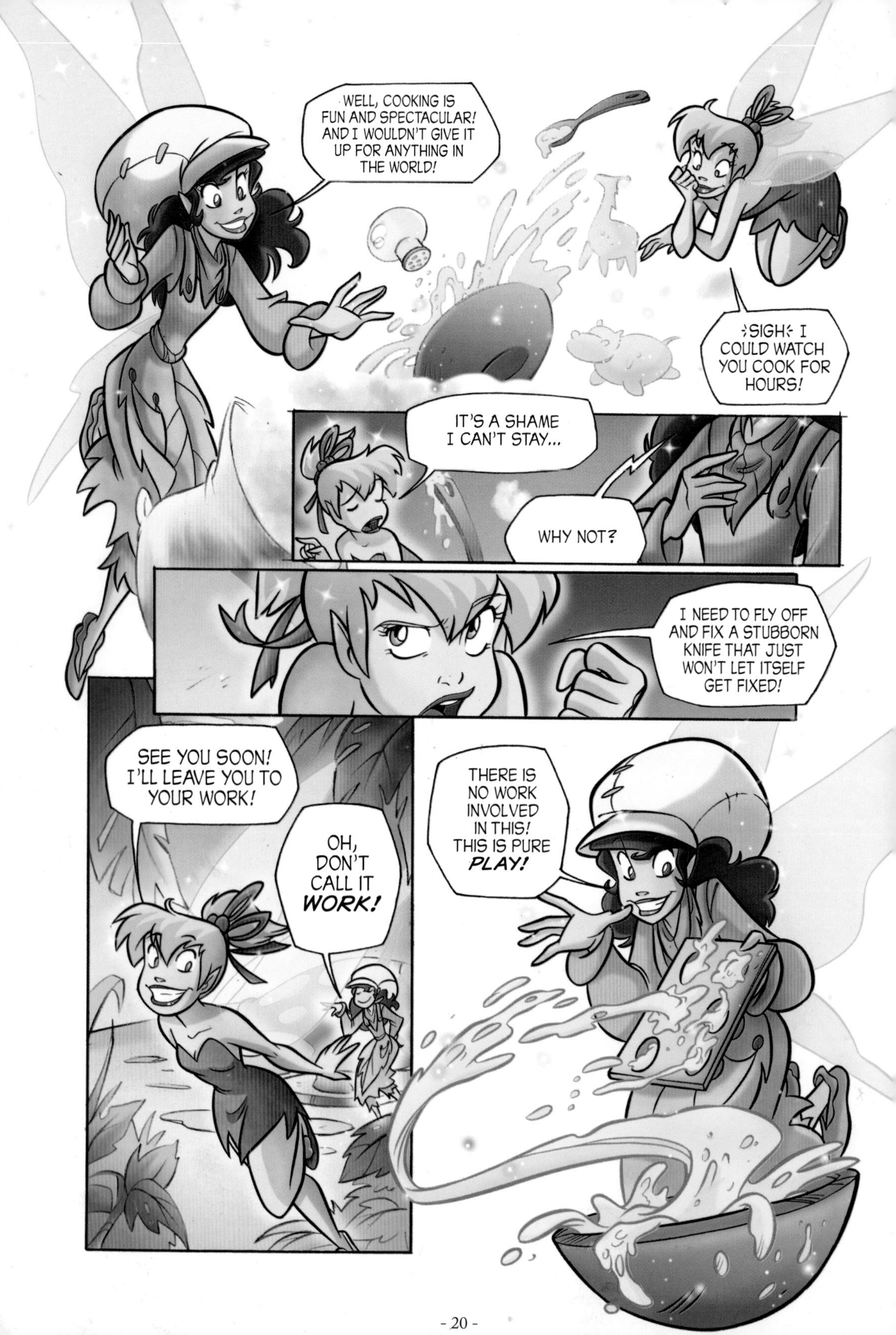
WELL, COOKING IS FUN AND SPECTACULAR! AND I WOULDN'T GIVE IT UP FOR ANYTHING IN THE WORLD!
⁏SIGH⁏ I COULD WATCH YOU COOK FOR HOURS!
IT'S A SHAME I CAN'T STAY...
WHY NOT?
I NEED TO FLY OFF AND FIX A STUBBORN KNIFE THAT JUST WON'T LET ITSELF GET FIXED!
SEE YOU SOON! I'LL LEAVE YOU TO YOUR WORK!
OH, DON'T CALL IT WORK!
THERE IS NO WORK INVOLVED IN THIS! THIS IS PURE PLAY!

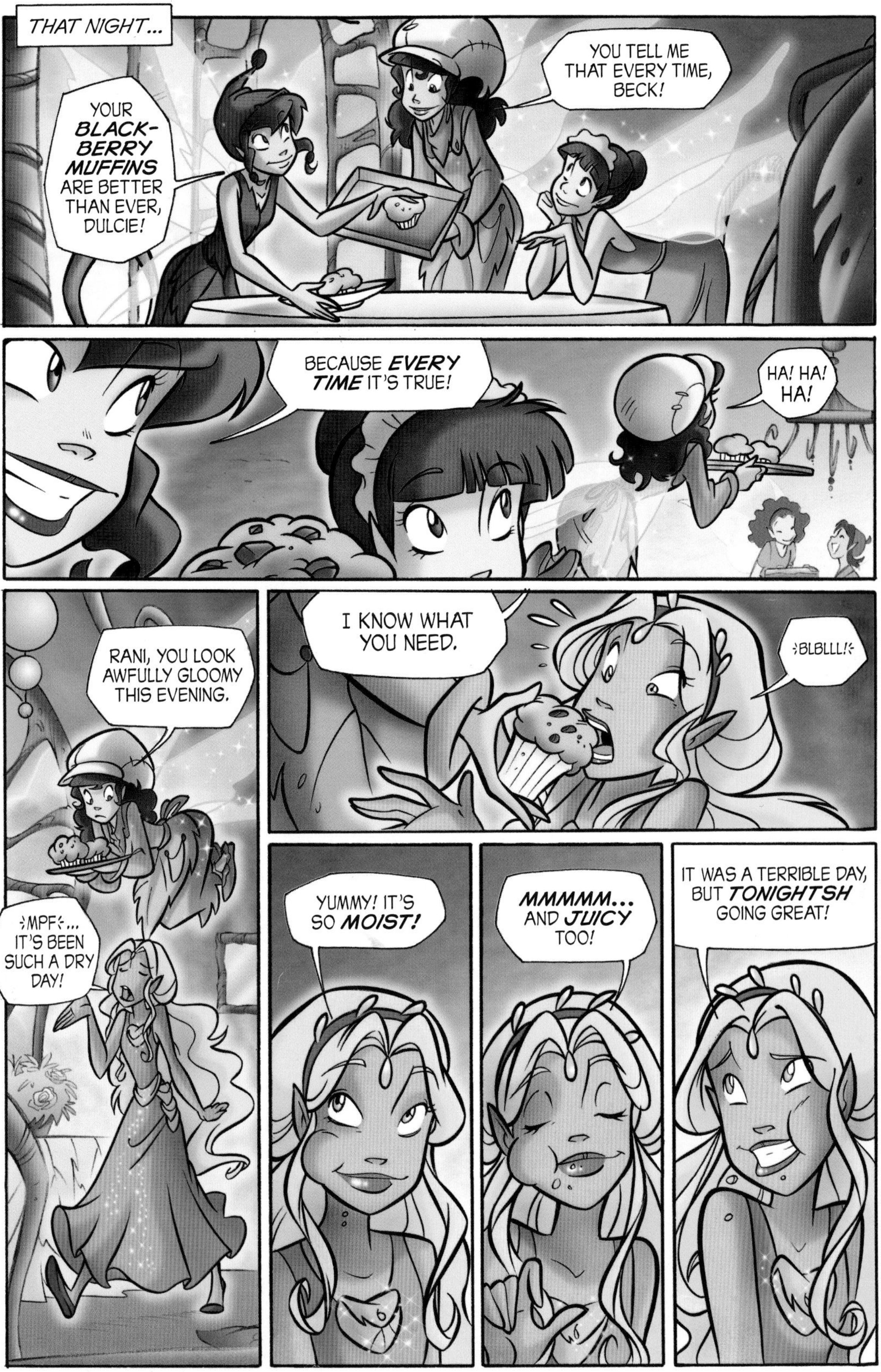
THAT NIGHT...
YOUR BLACK-BERRY MUFFINS ARE BETTER THAN EVER, DULCIE!
YOU TELL ME THAT EVERY TIME, BECK!
BECAUSE EVERY TIME IT'S TRUE!
HA! HA! HA!
RANI, YOU LOOK AWFULLY GLOOMY THIS EVENING.
MPF... IT'S BEEN SUCH A DRY DAY!
I KNOW WHAT YOU NEED.
BLBLLL!
YUMMY! IT'S SO MOIST!
MMMMM... AND JUICY TOO!
IT WAS A TERRIBLE DAY, BUT TONIGHTSH GOING GREAT!

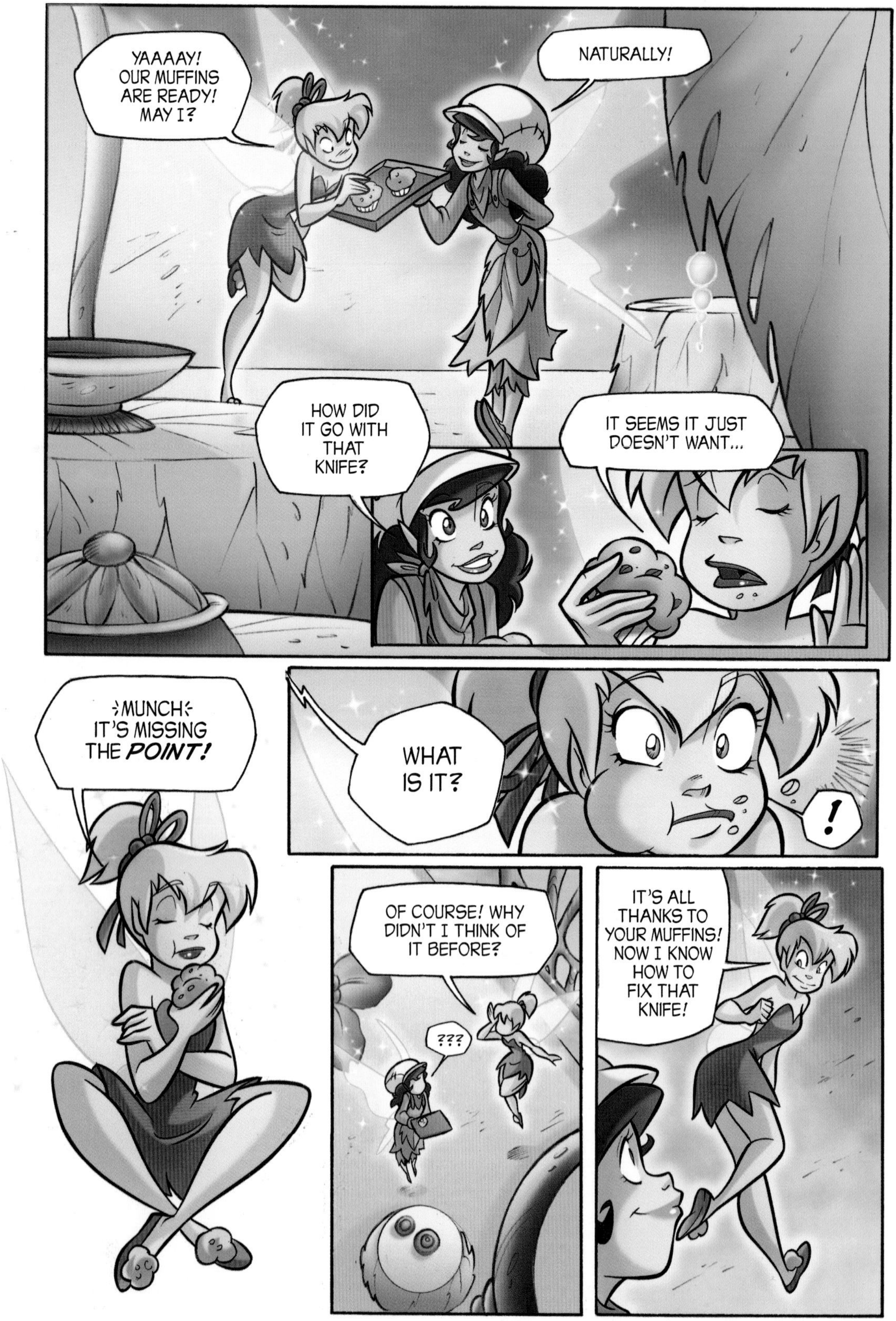
YAAAAY! OUR MUFFINS ARE READY! MAY I?
NATURALLY!
HOW DID IT GO WITH THAT KNIFE?
IT SEEMS IT JUST DOESN'T WANT...
MUNCH
IT'S MISSING THE *POINT!*
WHAT IS IT?
!
OF COURSE! WHY DIDN'T I THINK OF IT BEFORE?
???
IT'S ALL THANKS TO YOUR MUFFINS! NOW I KNOW HOW TO FIX THAT KNIFE!

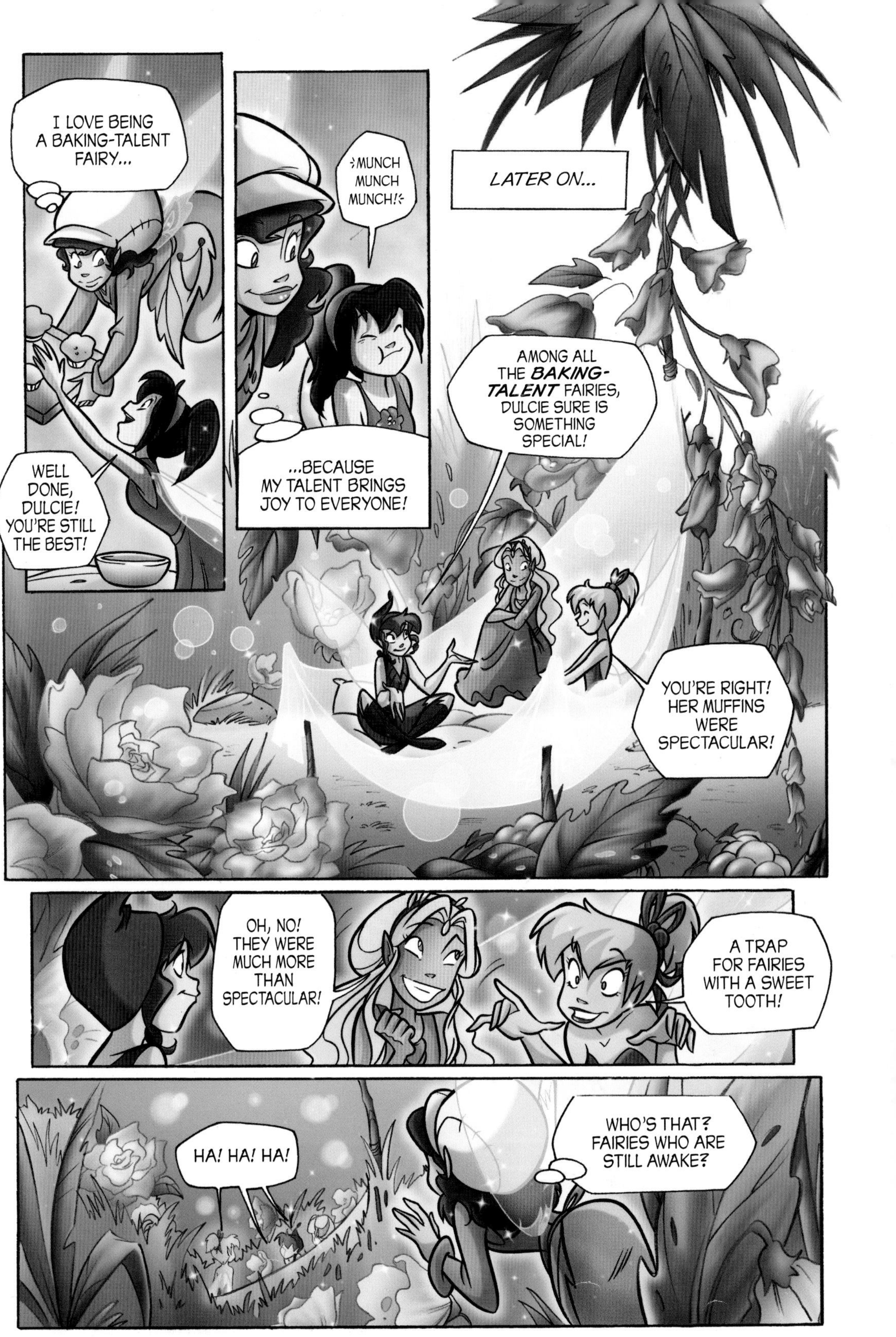
I LOVE BEING A BAKING-TALENT FAIRY...
WELL DONE, DULCIE! YOU'RE STILL THE BEST!
MUNCH MUNCH MUNCH!
...BECAUSE MY TALENT BRINGS JOY TO EVERYONE!
LATER ON...
AMONG ALL THE BAKING-TALENT FAIRIES, DULCIE SURE IS SOMETHING SPECIAL!
YOU'RE RIGHT! HER MUFFINS WERE SPECTACULAR!
OH, NO! THEY WERE MUCH MORE THAN SPECTACULAR!
A TRAP FOR FAIRIES WITH A SWEET TOOTH!
HA! HA! HA!
WHO'S THAT? FAIRIES WHO ARE STILL AWAKE?

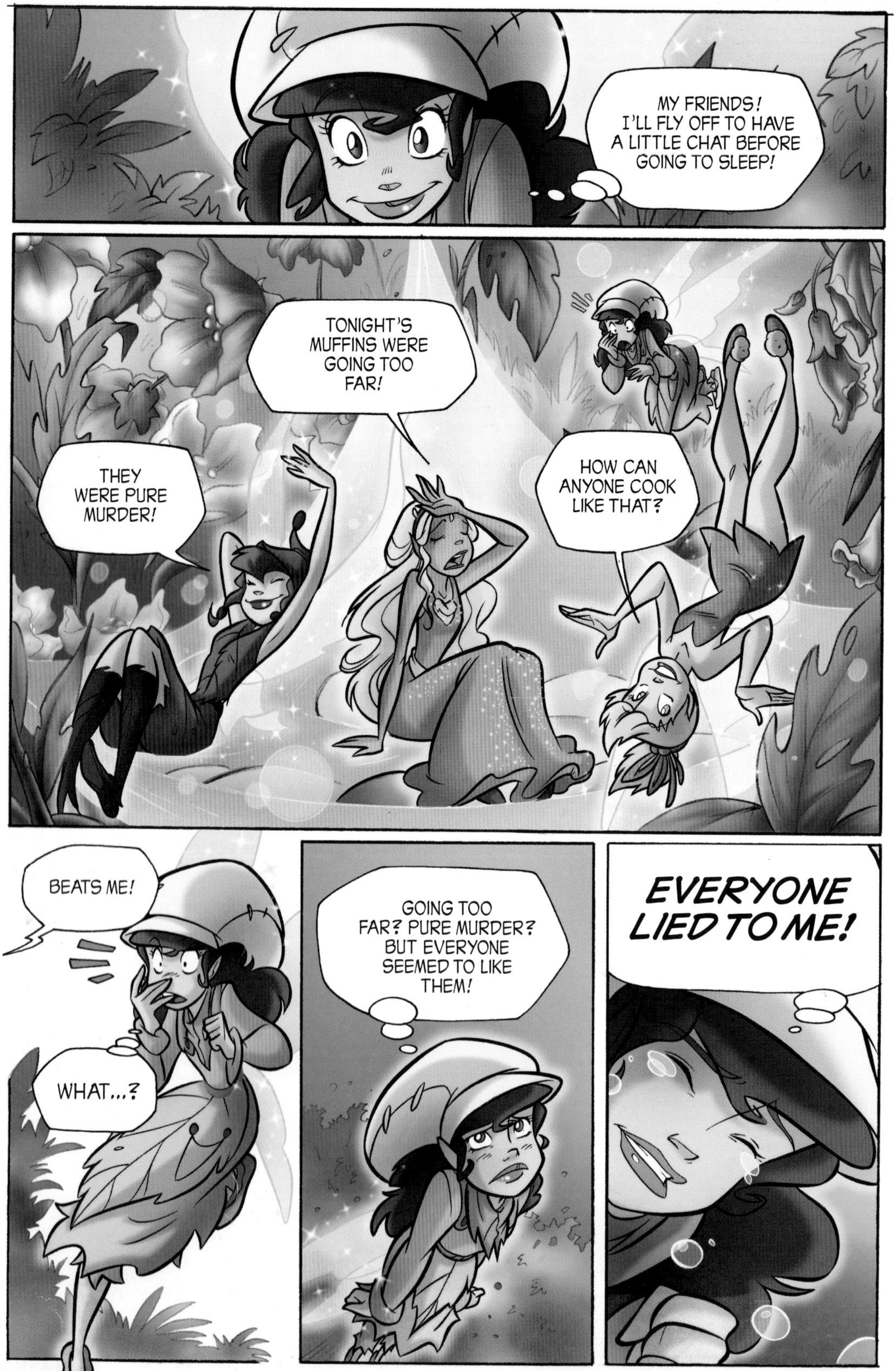
MY FRIENDS! I'LL FLY OFF TO HAVE A LITTLE CHAT BEFORE GOING TO SLEEP!
TONIGHT'S MUFFINS WERE GOING TOO FAR!
THEY WERE PURE MURDER!
HOW CAN ANYONE COOK LIKE THAT?
BEATS ME!
WHAT...?
GOING TOO FAR? PURE MURDER? BUT EVERYONE SEEMED TO LIKE THEM!
EVERYONE LIED TO ME!

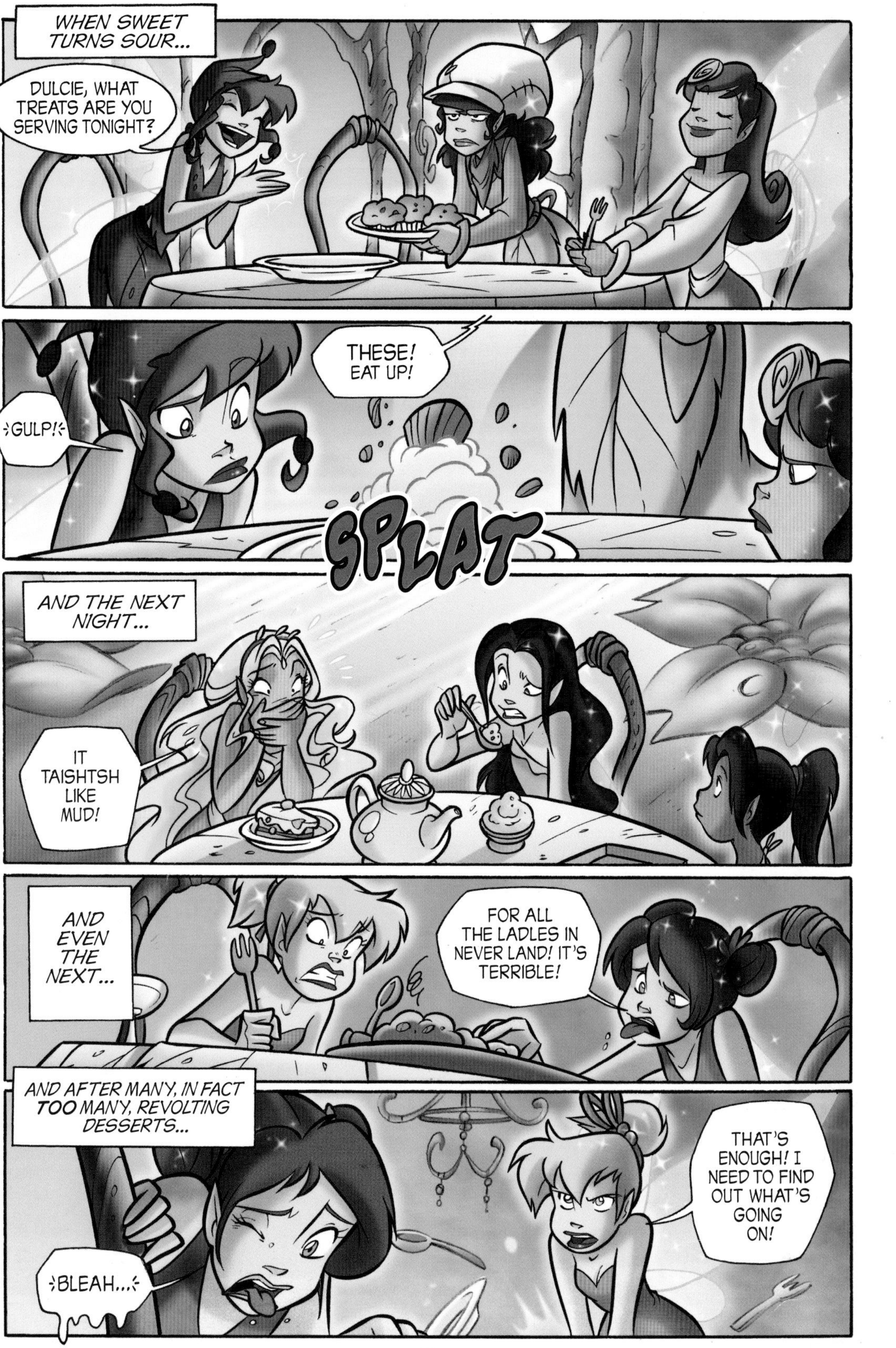
WHEN SWEET TURNS SOUR...
DULCIE, WHAT TREATS ARE YOU SERVING TONIGHT?
THESE! EAT UP!
GULP!
SPLAT
AND THE NEXT NIGHT...
IT TAISHTSH LIKE MUD!
AND EVEN THE NEXT...
FOR ALL THE LADLES IN NEVER LAND! IT'S TERRIBLE!
AND AFTER MANY, IN FACT TOO MANY, REVOLTING DESSERTS...
BLEAH...
THAT'S ENOUGH! I NEED TO FIND OUT WHAT'S GOING ON!

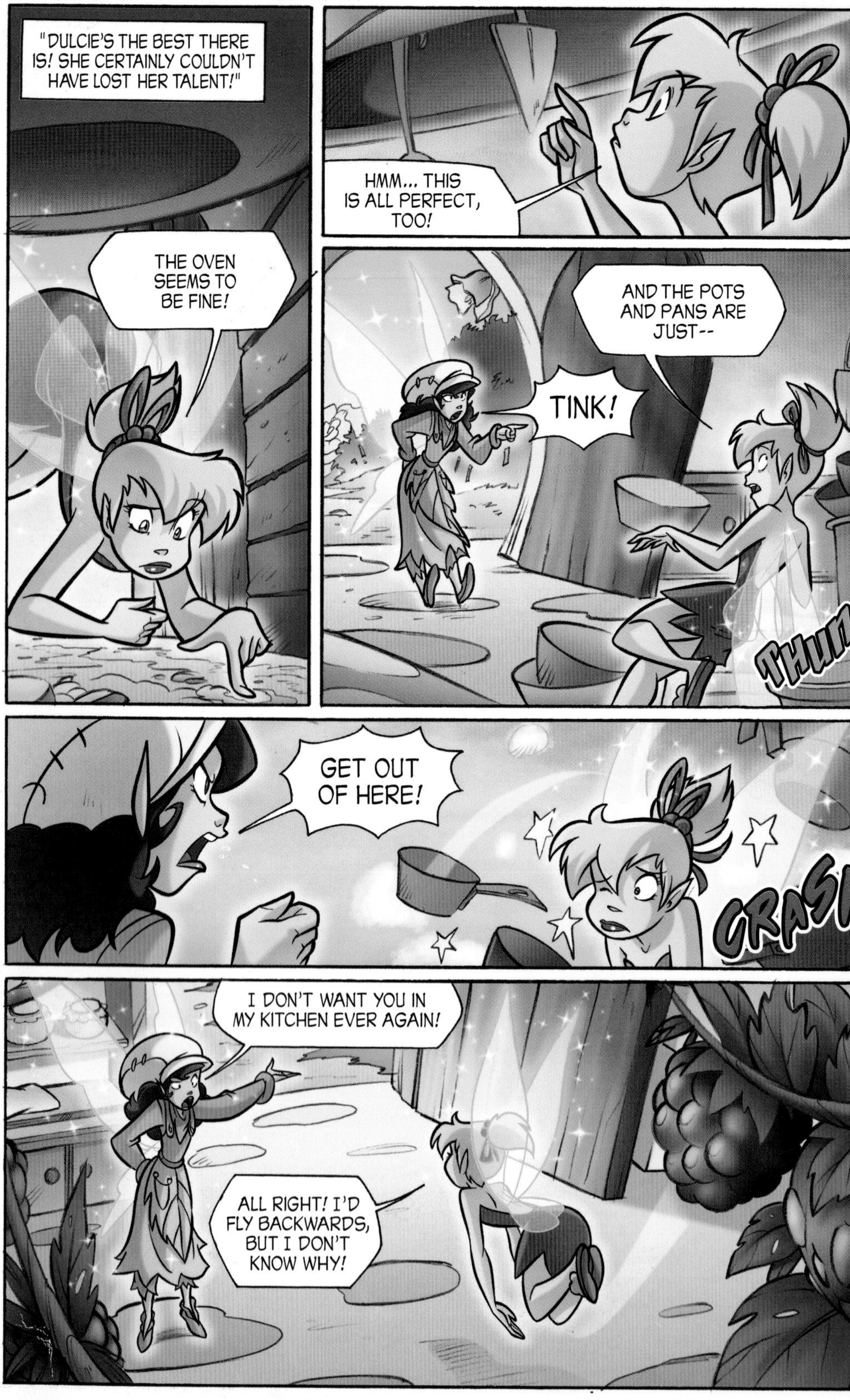
"DULCIE'S THE BEST THERE IS! SHE CERTAINLY COULDN'T HAVE LOST HER TALENT!"
HMM... THIS IS ALL PERFECT, TOO!
THE OVEN SEEMS TO BE FINE!
AND THE POTS AND PANS ARE JUST--
TINK!
THUNK
GET OUT OF HERE!
CRASH
I DON'T WANT YOU IN MY KITCHEN EVER AGAIN!
ALL RIGHT! I'D FLY BACKWARDS, BUT I DON'T KNOW WHY!

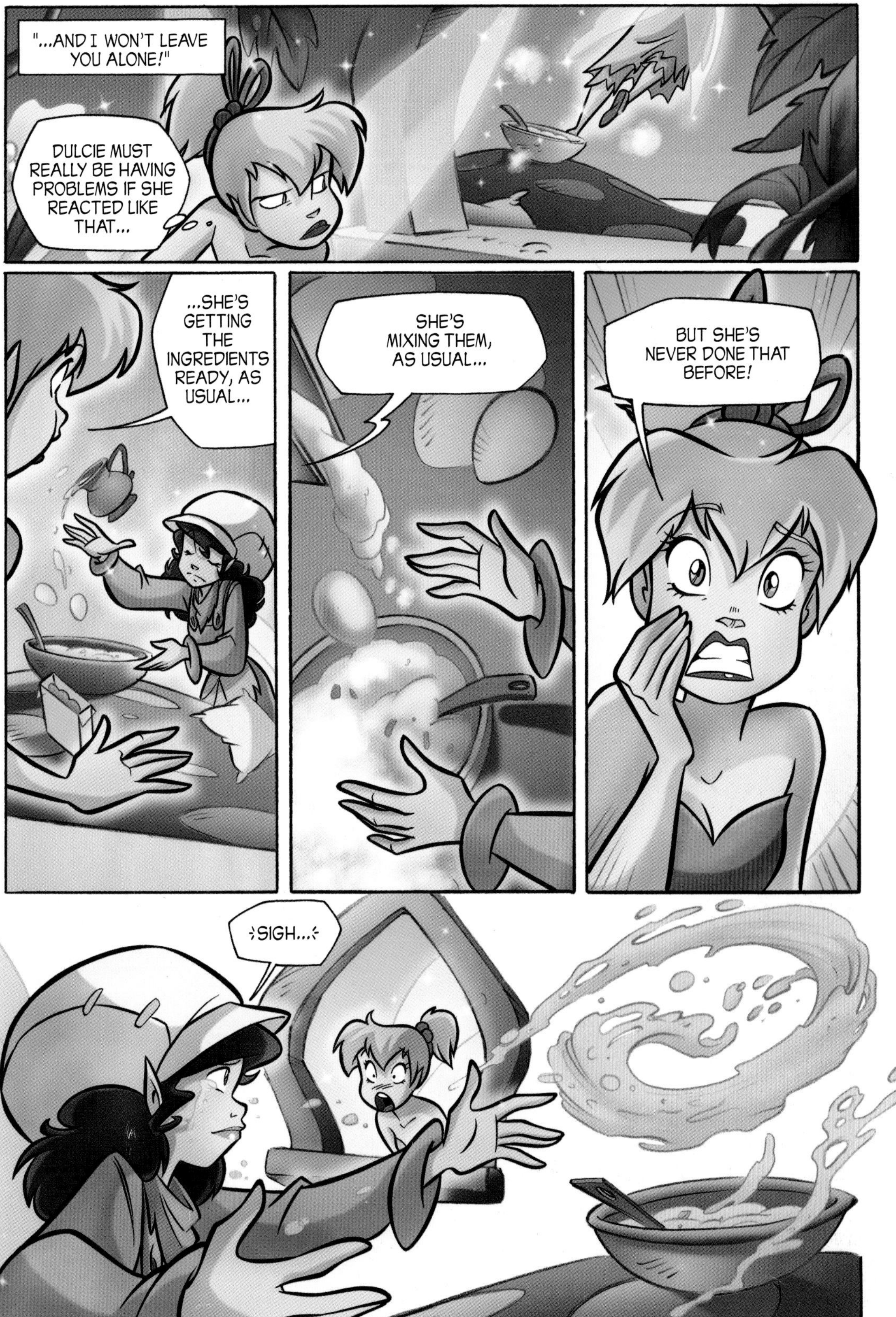
"...AND I WON'T LEAVE YOU ALONE!"
DULCIE MUST REALLY BE HAVING PROBLEMS IF SHE REACTED LIKE THAT...
...SHE'S GETTING THE INGREDIENTS READY, AS USUAL...
SHE'S MIXING THEM, AS USUAL...
BUT SHE'S NEVER DONE THAT BEFORE!
SIGH...

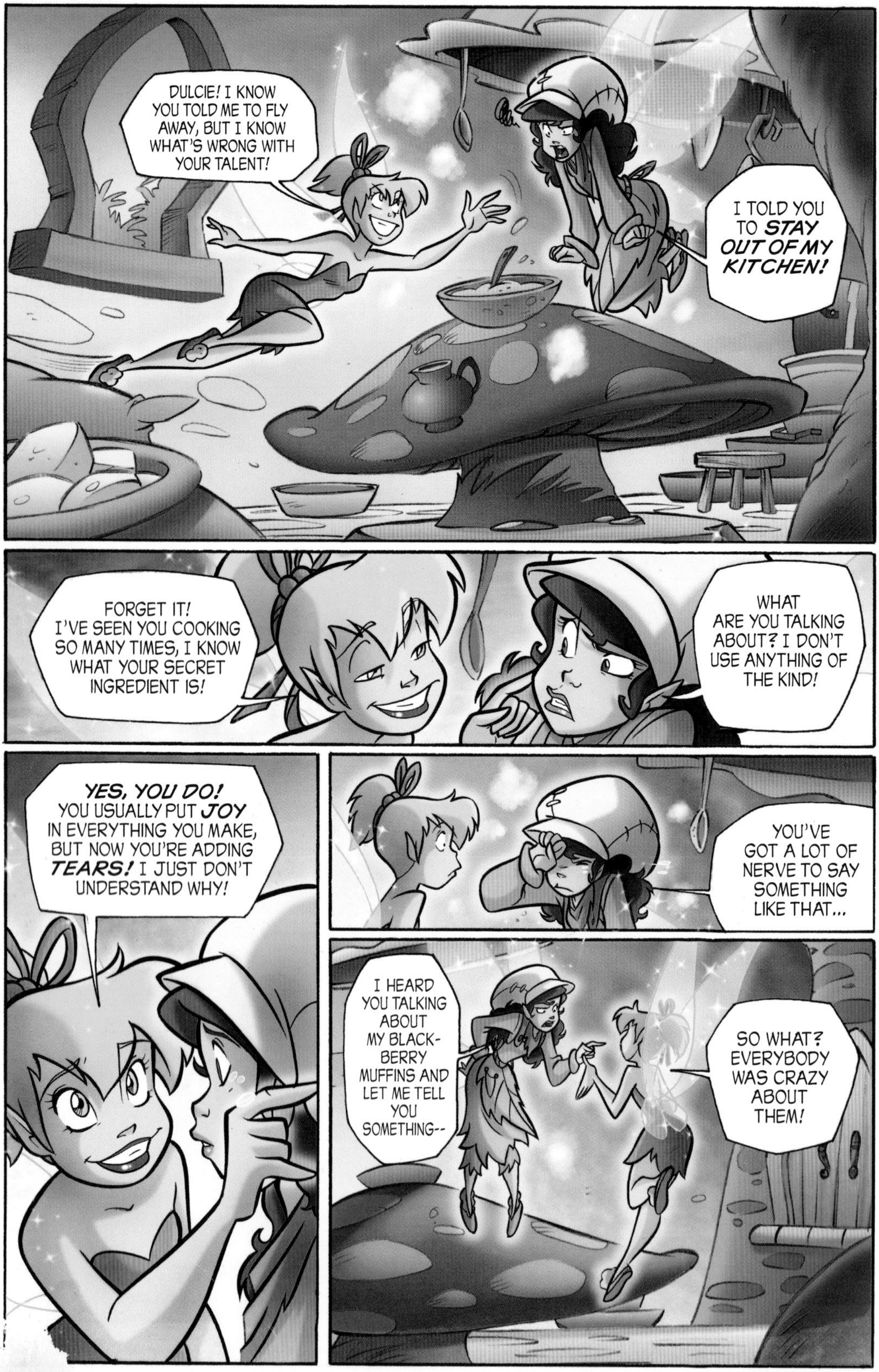
DULCIE! I KNOW YOU TOLD ME TO FLY AWAY, BUT I KNOW WHAT'S WRONG WITH YOUR TALENT!
I TOLD YOU TO STAY OUT OF MY KITCHEN!
FORGET IT! I'VE SEEN YOU COOKING SO MANY TIMES, I KNOW WHAT YOUR SECRET INGREDIENT IS!
WHAT ARE YOU TALKING ABOUT? I DON'T USE ANYTHING OF THE KIND!
YES, YOU DO! YOU USUALLY PUT JOY IN EVERYTHING YOU MAKE, BUT NOW YOU'RE ADDING TEARS! I JUST DON'T UNDERSTAND WHY!
YOU'VE GOT A LOT OF NERVE TO SAY SOMETHING LIKE THAT...
I HEARD YOU TALKING ABOUT MY BLACK-BERRY MUFFINS AND LET ME TELL YOU SOMETHING--
SO WHAT? EVERYBODY WAS CRAZY ABOUT THEM!

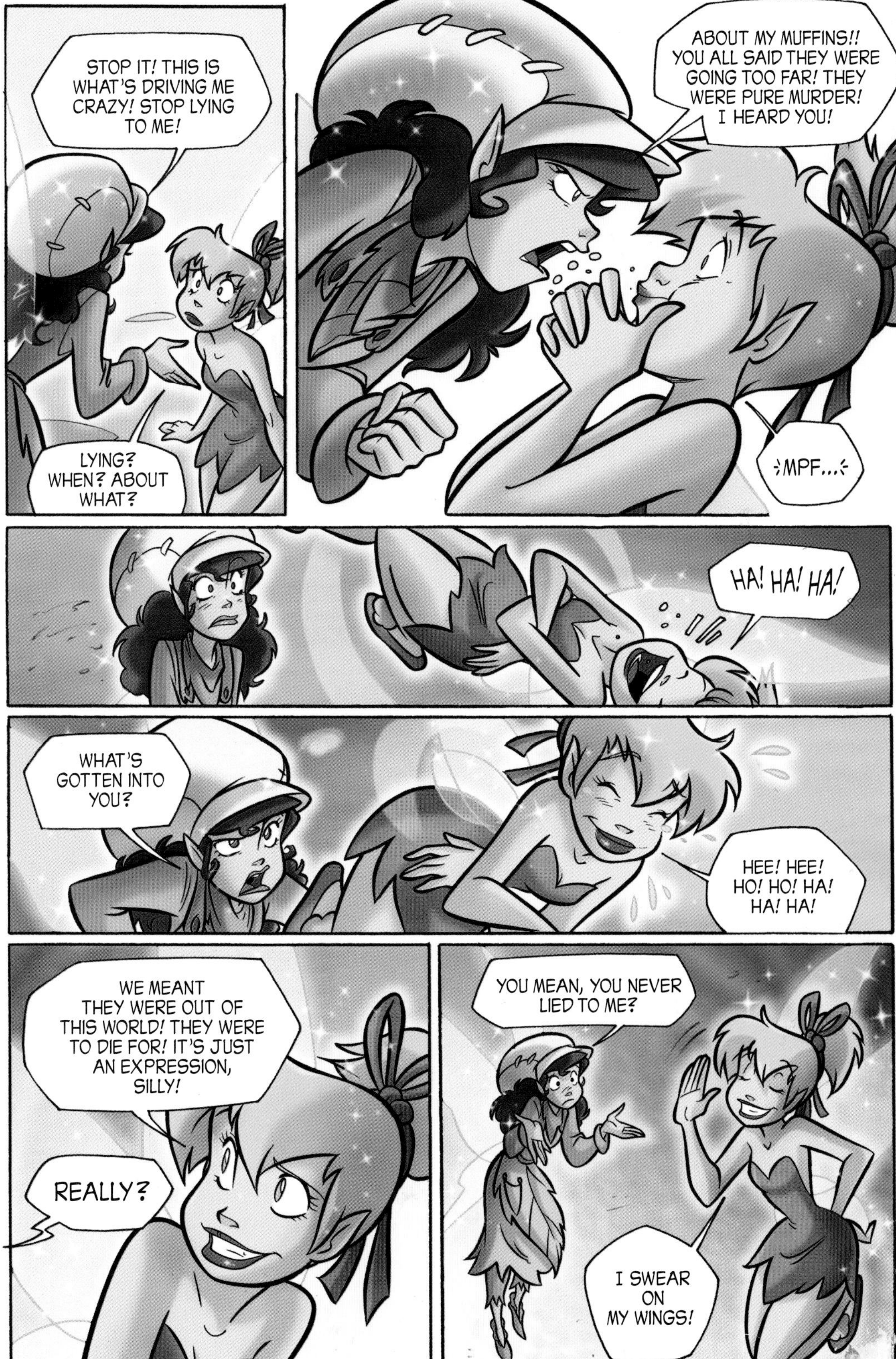
STOP IT! THIS IS WHAT'S DRIVING ME CRAZY! STOP LYING TO ME!
LYING? WHEN? ABOUT WHAT?
ABOUT MY MUFFINS!! YOU ALL SAID THEY WERE GOING TOO FAR! THEY WERE PURE MURDER! I HEARD YOU!
MPF...
HA! HA! HA!
WHAT'S GOTTEN INTO YOU?
HEE! HEE! HO! HO! HA! HA! HA!
WE MEANT THEY WERE OUT OF THIS WORLD! THEY WERE TO DIE FOR! IT'S JUST AN EXPRESSION, SILLY!
REALLY?
YOU MEAN, YOU NEVER LIED TO ME?
I SWEAR ON MY WINGS!

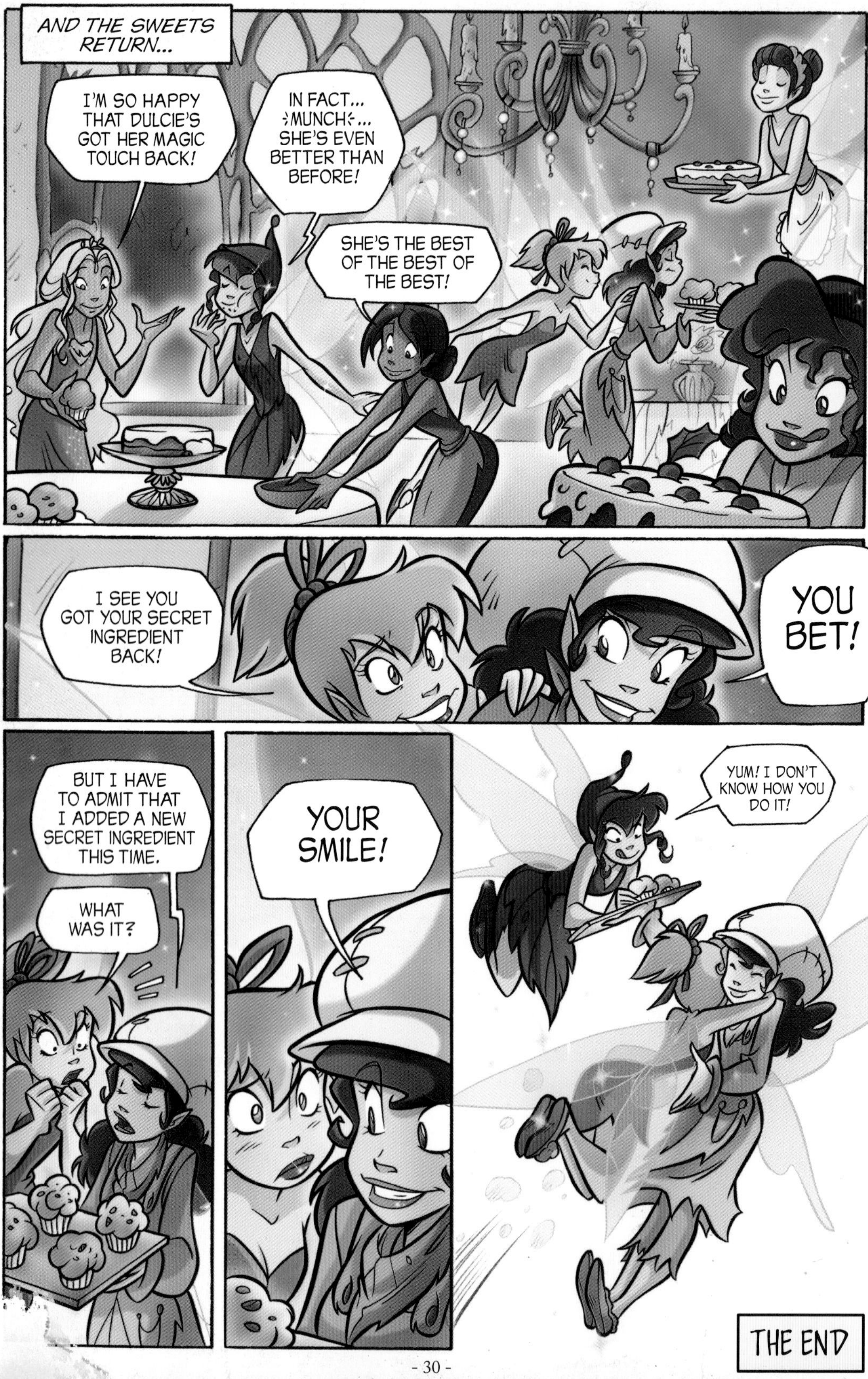
AND THE SWEETS RETURN...
I'M SO HAPPY THAT DULCIE'S GOT HER MAGIC TOUCH BACK!
IN FACT... ⁝MUNCH⁝... SHE'S EVEN BETTER THAN BEFORE!
SHE'S THE BEST OF THE BEST OF THE BEST!
I SEE YOU GOT YOUR SECRET INGREDIENT BACK!
YOU BET!
BUT I HAVE TO ADMIT THAT I ADDED A NEW SECRET INGREDIENT THIS TIME.
WHAT WAS IT?
YOUR SMILE!
YUM! I DON'T KNOW HOW YOU DO IT!
THE END

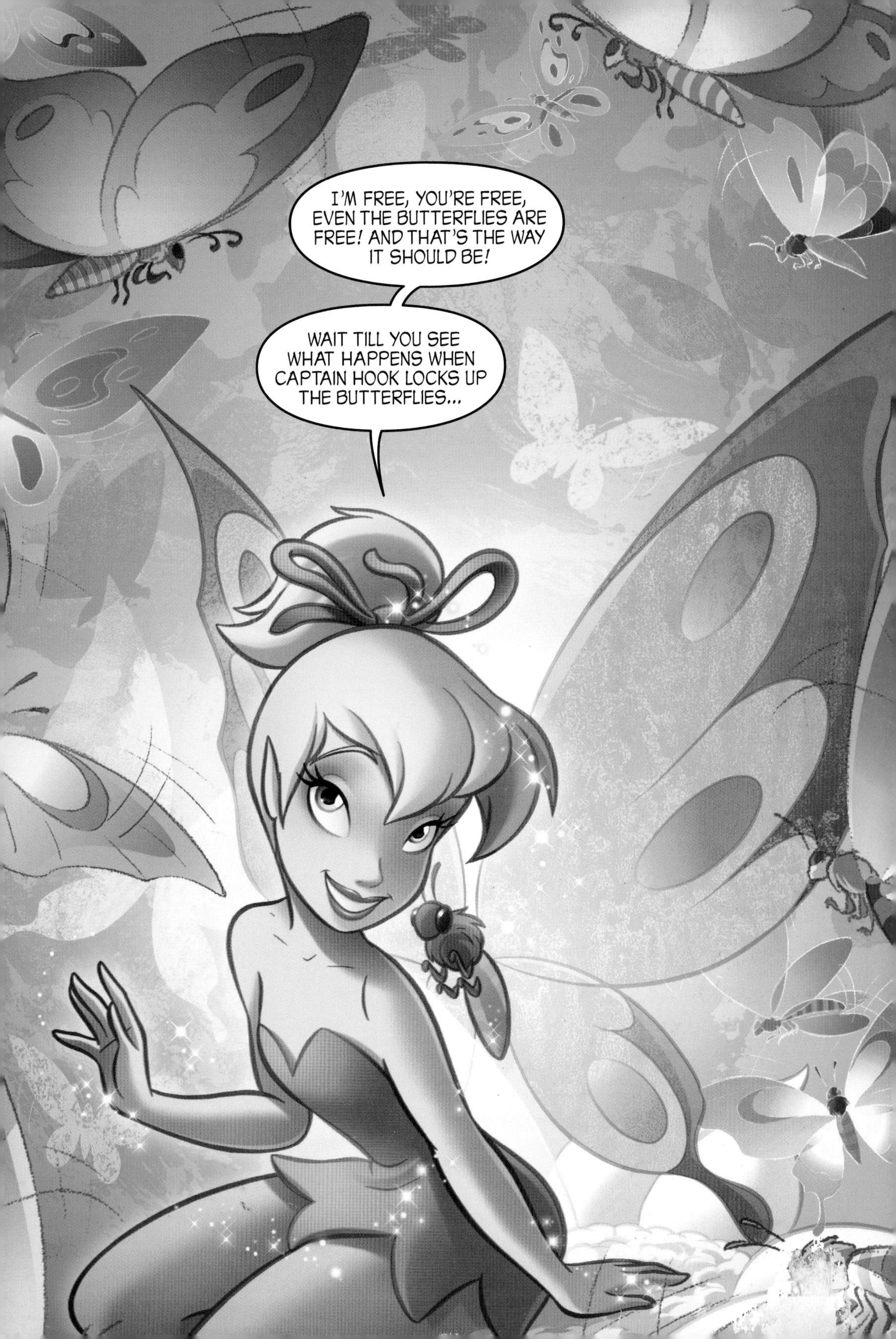
I'M FREE, YOU'RE FREE, EVEN THE BUTTERFLIES ARE FREE! AND THAT'S THE WAY IT SHOULD BE!
WAIT TILL YOU SEE WHAT HAPPENS WHEN CAPTAIN HOOK LOCKS UP THE BUTTERFLIES...

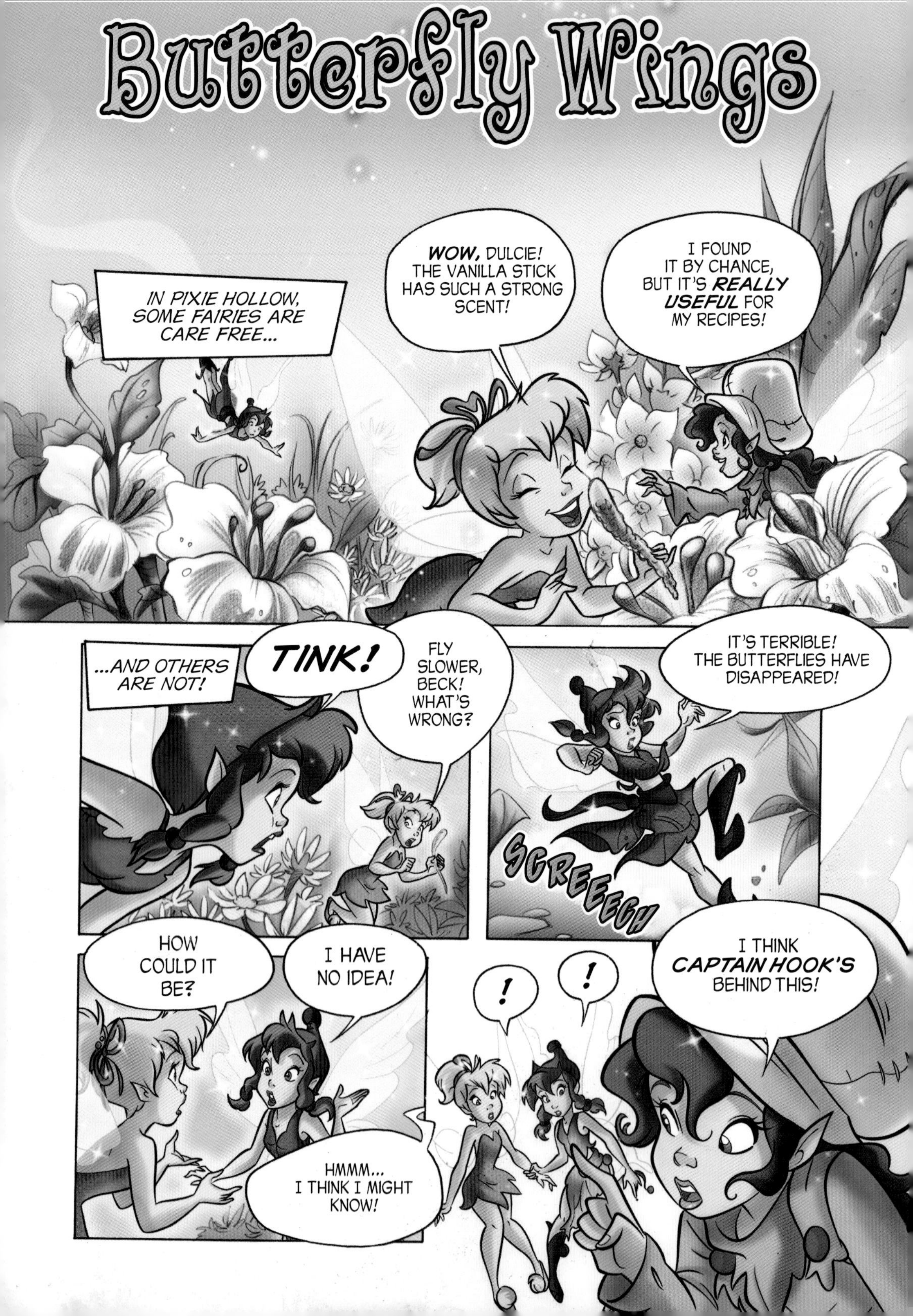
Butterfly Wings
IN PIXIE HOLLOW, SOME FAIRIES ARE CARE FREE...
WOW, DULCIE! THE VANILLA STICK HAS SUCH A STRONG SCENT!
I FOUND IT BY CHANCE, BUT IT'S REALLY USEFUL FOR MY RECIPES!
...AND OTHERS ARE NOT!
TINK!
FLY SLOWER, BECK! WHAT'S WRONG?
IT'S TERRIBLE! THE BUTTERFLIES HAVE DISAPPEARED!
SCREEECH
HOW COULD IT BE?
I HAVE NO IDEA!
HMMM... I THINK I MIGHT KNOW!
!
!
I THINK CAPTAIN HOOK'S BEHIND THIS!

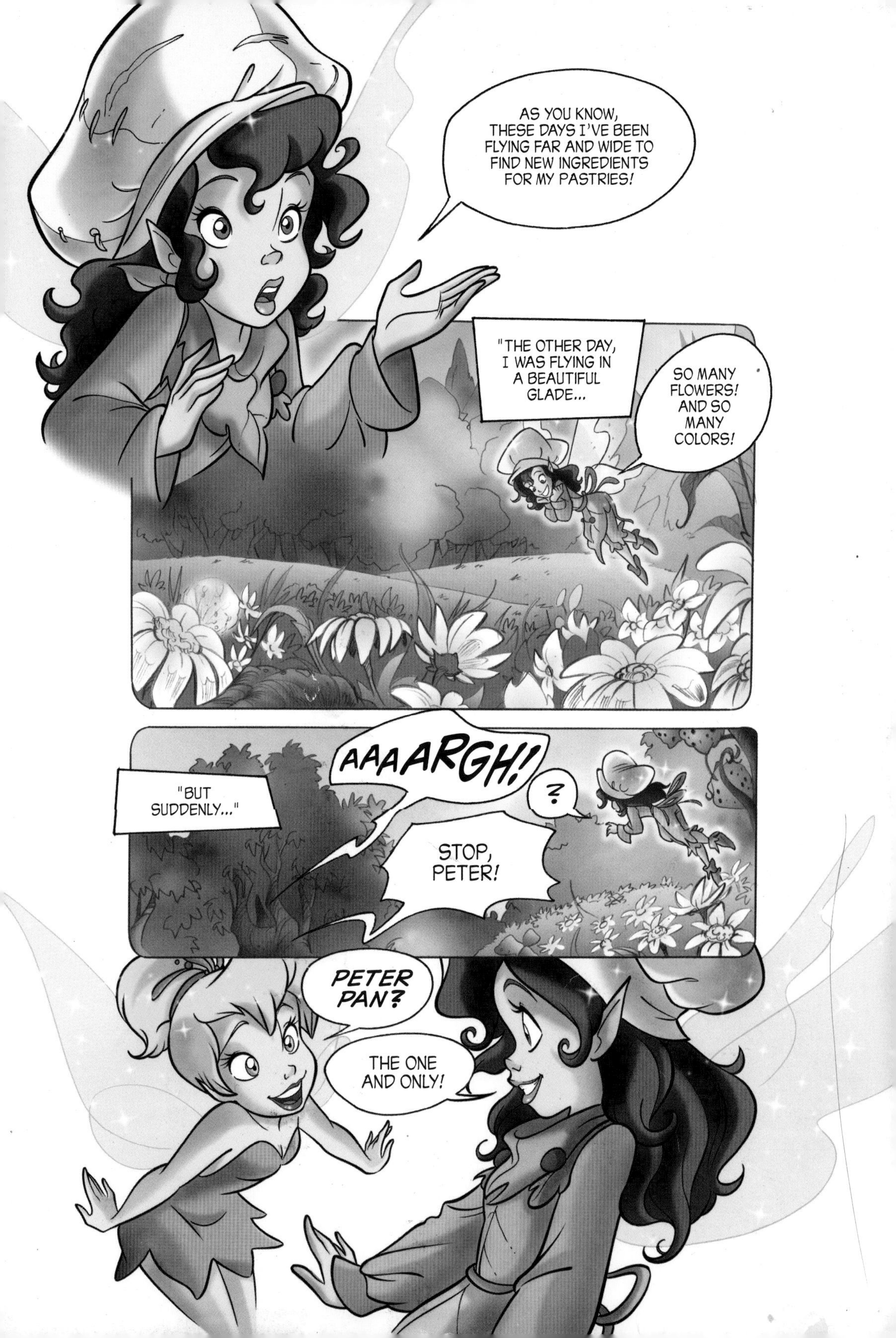
AS YOU KNOW, THESE DAYS I'VE BEEN FLYING FAR AND WIDE TO FIND NEW INGREDIENTS FOR MY PASTRIES!
"THE OTHER DAY, I WAS FLYING IN A BEAUTIFUL GLADE...
SO MANY FLOWERS! AND SO MANY COLORS!
"BUT SUDDENLY..."
AAAARGH!
?
STOP, PETER!
PETER PAN?
THE ONE AND ONLY!

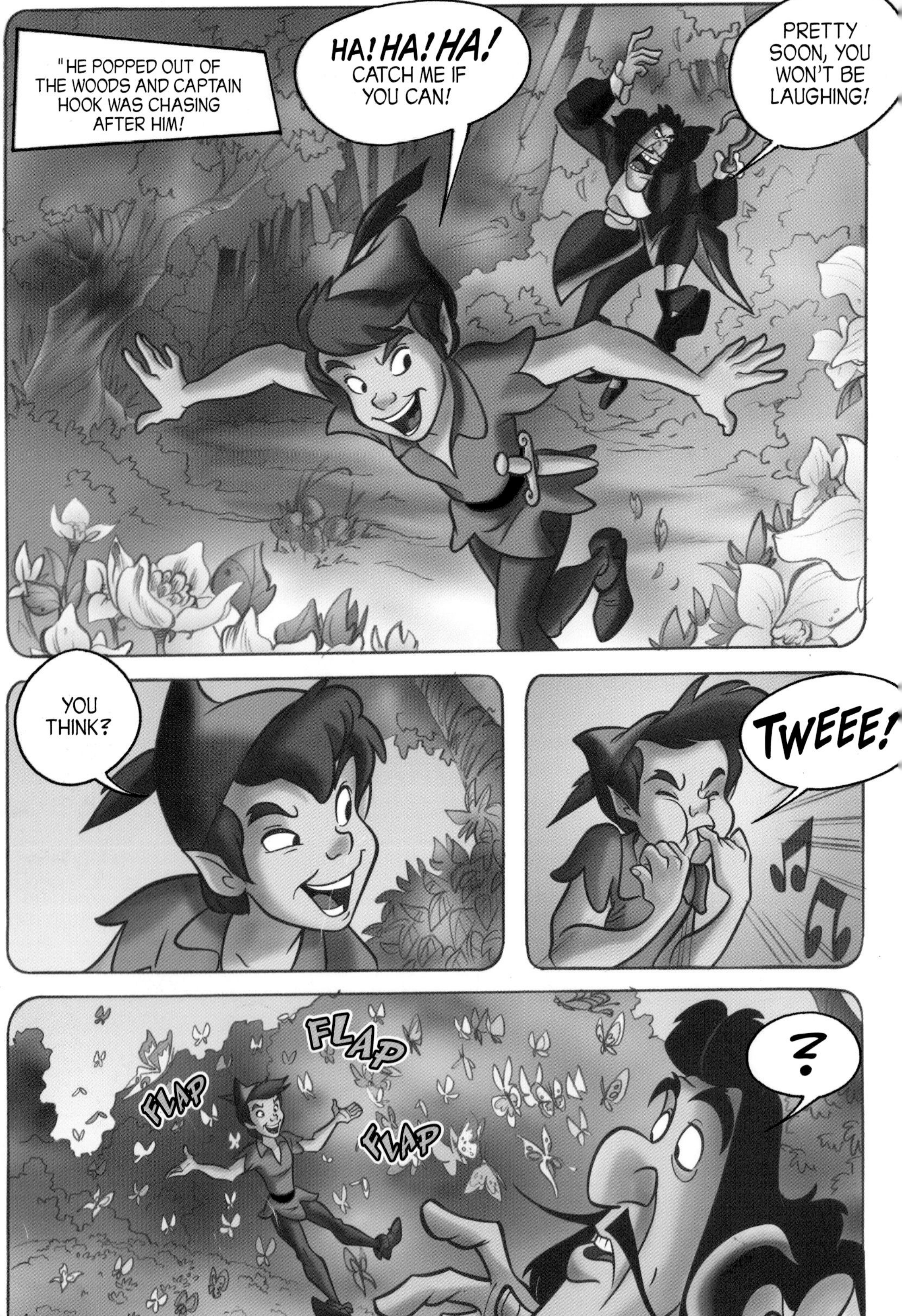

"HE POPPED OUT OF THE WOODS AND CAPTAIN HOOK WAS CHASING AFTER HIM!
HA! HA! HA! CATCH ME IF YOU CAN!
PRETTY SOON, YOU WON'T BE LAUGHING!
YOU THINK?
TWEEE!
FLAP
FLAP
FLAP
?

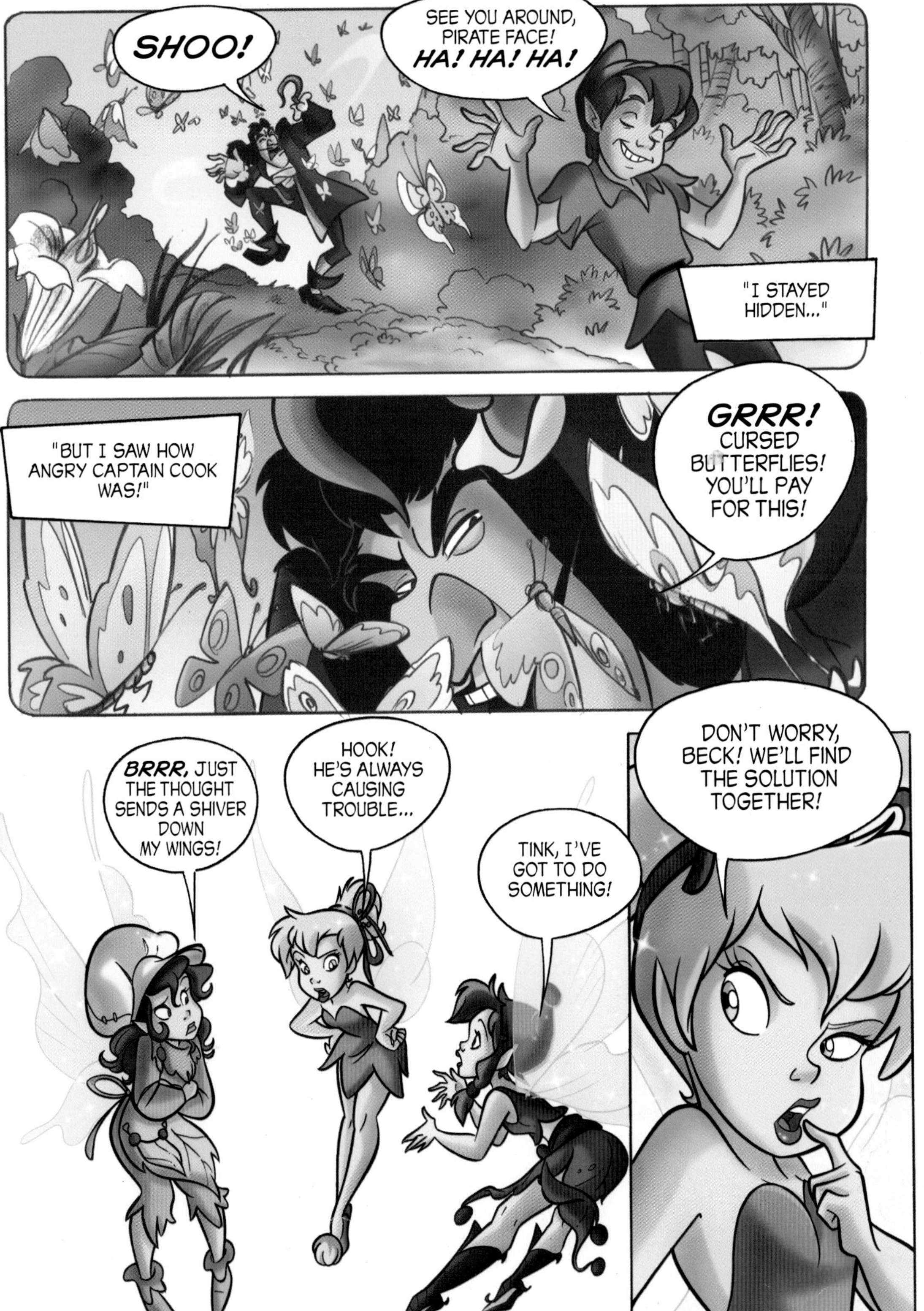

SHOO!
SEE YOU AROUND, PIRATE FACE! HA! HA! HA!
"I STAYED HIDDEN..."
"BUT I SAW HOW ANGRY CAPTAIN COOK WAS!"
GRRR! CURSED BUTTERFLIES! YOU'LL PAY FOR THIS!
BRRR, JUST THE THOUGHT SENDS A SHIVER DOWN MY WINGS!
HOOK! HE'S ALWAYS CAUSING TROUBLE...
TINK, I'VE GOT TO DO SOMETHING!
DON'T WORRY, BECK! WE'LL FIND THE SOLUTION TOGETHER!

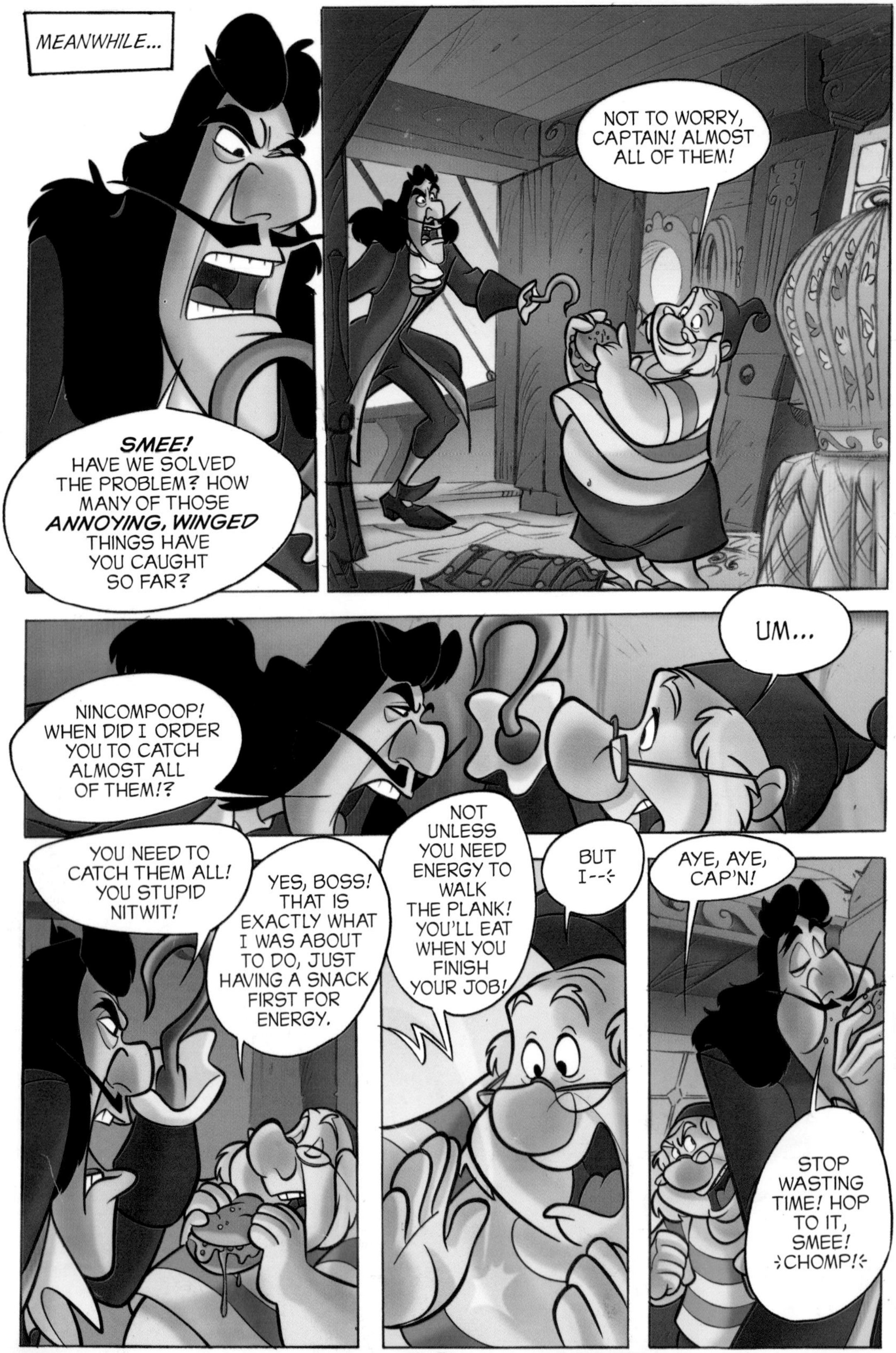

MEANWHILE...
SMEE! HAVE WE SOLVED THE PROBLEM? HOW MANY OF THOSE ANNOYING, WINGED THINGS HAVE YOU CAUGHT SO FAR?
NOT TO WORRY, CAPTAIN! ALMOST ALL OF THEM!
UM...
NINCOMPOOP! WHEN DID I ORDER YOU TO CATCH ALMOST ALL OF THEM!?
YOU NEED TO CATCH THEM ALL! YOU STUPID NITWIT!
YES, BOSS! THAT IS EXACTLY WHAT I WAS ABOUT TO DO, JUST HAVING A SNACK FIRST FOR ENERGY.
NOT UNLESS YOU NEED ENERGY TO WALK THE PLANK! YOU'LL EAT WHEN YOU FINISH YOUR JOB!
BUT I--
AYE, AYE, CAP'N!
STOP WASTING TIME! HOP TO IT, SMEE! CHOMP!

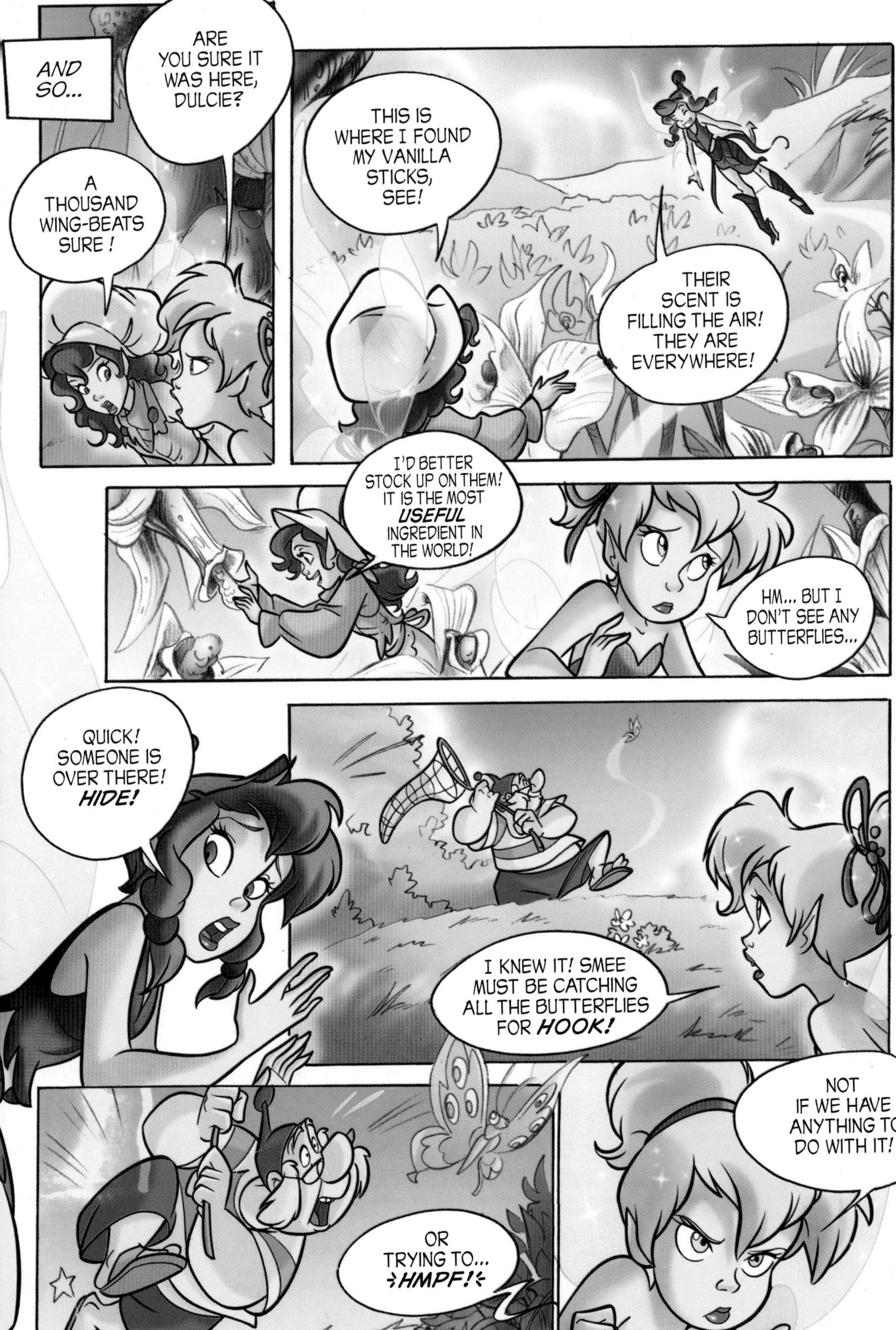
AND SO...
ARE YOU SURE IT WAS HERE, DULCIE?
A THOUSAND WING-BEATS SURE !
THIS IS WHERE I FOUND MY VANILLA STICKS, SEE!
THEIR SCENT IS FILLING THE AIR! THEY ARE EVERYWHERE!
I'D BETTER STOCK UP ON THEM! IT IS THE MOST USEFUL INGREDIENT IN THE WORLD!
HM... BUT I DON'T SEE ANY BUTTERFLIES...
QUICK! SOMEONE IS OVER THERE! HIDE!
I KNEW IT! SMEE MUST BE CATCHING ALL THE BUTTERFLIES FOR HOOK!
OR TRYING TO... HMPF!
NOT IF WE HAVE ANYTHING TO DO WITH IT!

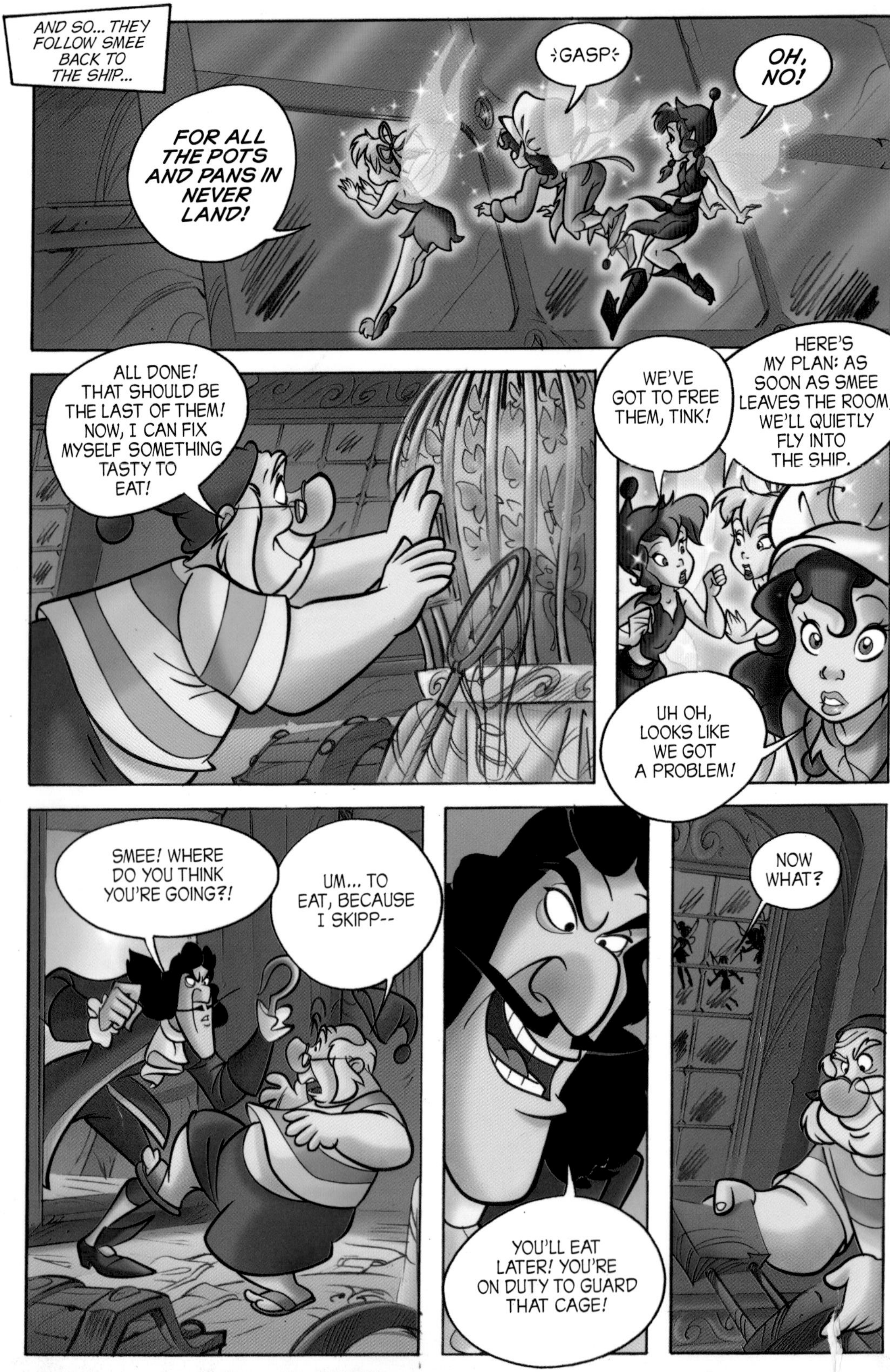
AND SO... THEY FOLLOW SMEE BACK TO THE SHIP...
FOR ALL THE POTS AND PANS IN NEVER LAND!
GASP
OH, NO!
ALL DONE! THAT SHOULD BE THE LAST OF THEM! NOW, I CAN FIX MYSELF SOMETHING TASTY TO EAT!
WE'VE GOT TO FREE THEM, TINK!
HERE'S MY PLAN: AS SOON AS SMEE LEAVES THE ROOM, WE'LL QUIETLY FLY INTO THE SHIP.
UH OH, LOOKS LIKE WE GOT A PROBLEM!
SMEE! WHERE DO YOU THINK YOU'RE GOING?!
UM... TO EAT, BECAUSE I SKIPP--
YOU'LL EAT LATER! YOU'RE ON DUTY TO GUARD THAT CAGE!
NOW WHAT?

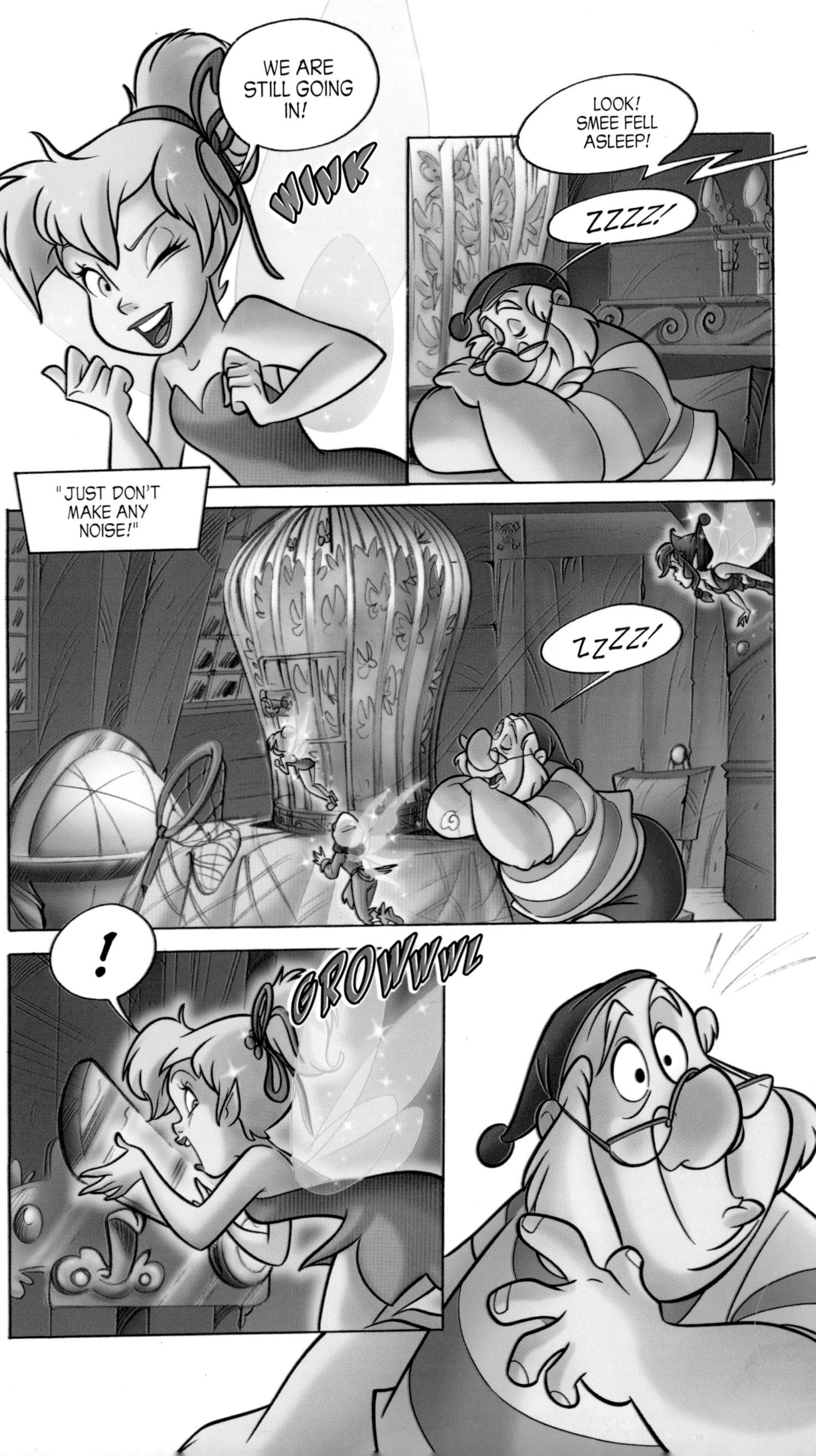

WE ARE STILL GOING IN!
WINK
LOOK! SMEE FELL ASLEEP!
ZZZZ!
"JUST DON'T MAKE ANY NOISE!"
ZZZZ!
!
GROWWWL

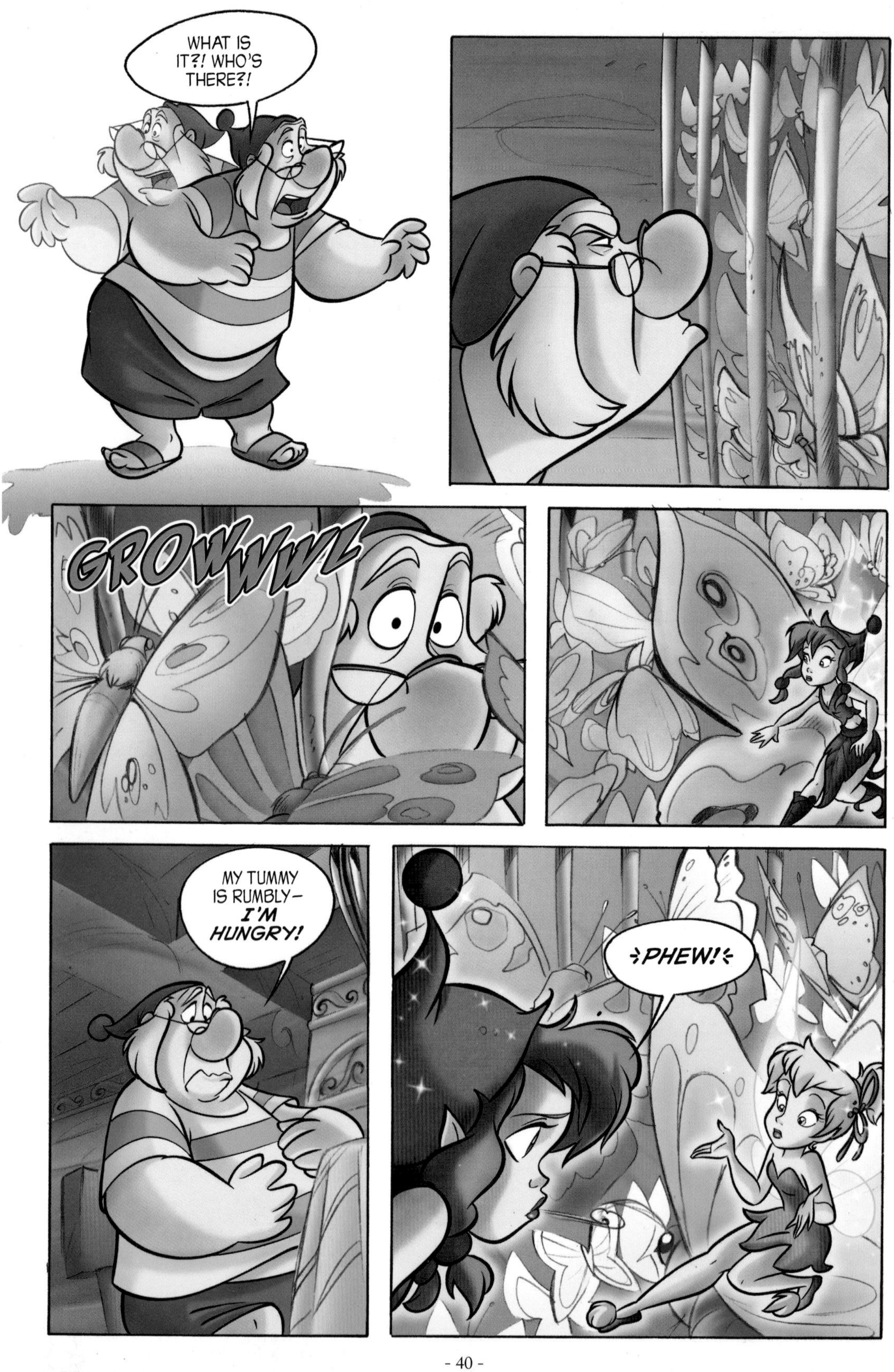
WHAT IS IT?! WHO'S THERE?!
GROWWWL
MY TUMMY IS RUMBLY— I'M HUNGRY!
PHEW!

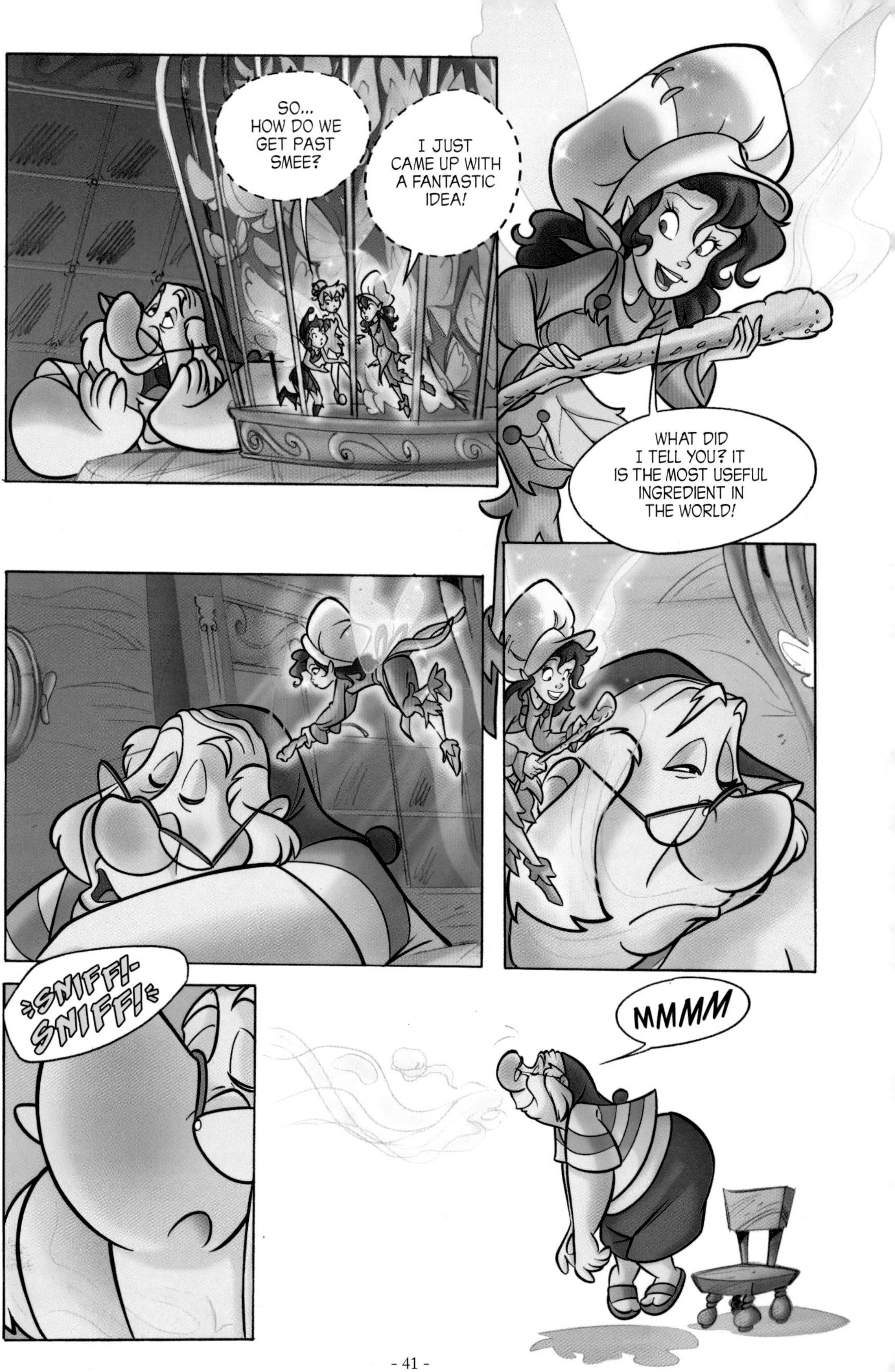
SO... HOW DO WE GET PAST SMEE?
I JUST CAME UP WITH A FANTASTIC IDEA!
WHAT DID I TELL YOU? IT IS THE MOST USEFUL INGREDIENT IN THE WORLD!
SNIFF! SNIFF!
MMMM

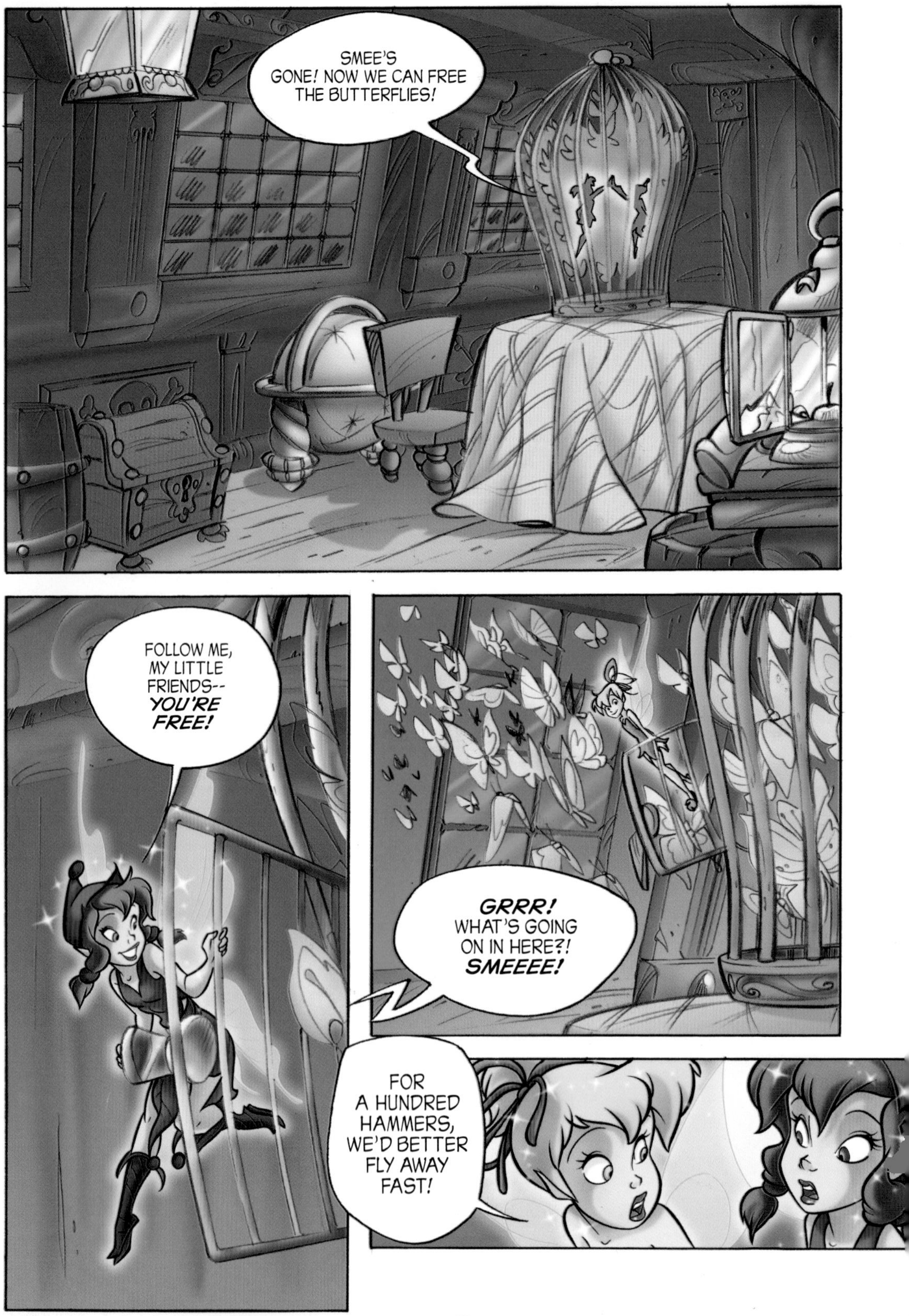
SMEE'S GONE! NOW WE CAN FREE THE BUTTERFLIES!
FOLLOW ME, MY LITTLE FRIENDS-- YOU'RE FREE!
GRRR! WHAT'S GOING ON IN HERE?! SMEEEE!
FOR A HUNDRED HAMMERS, WE'D BETTER FLY AWAY FAST!

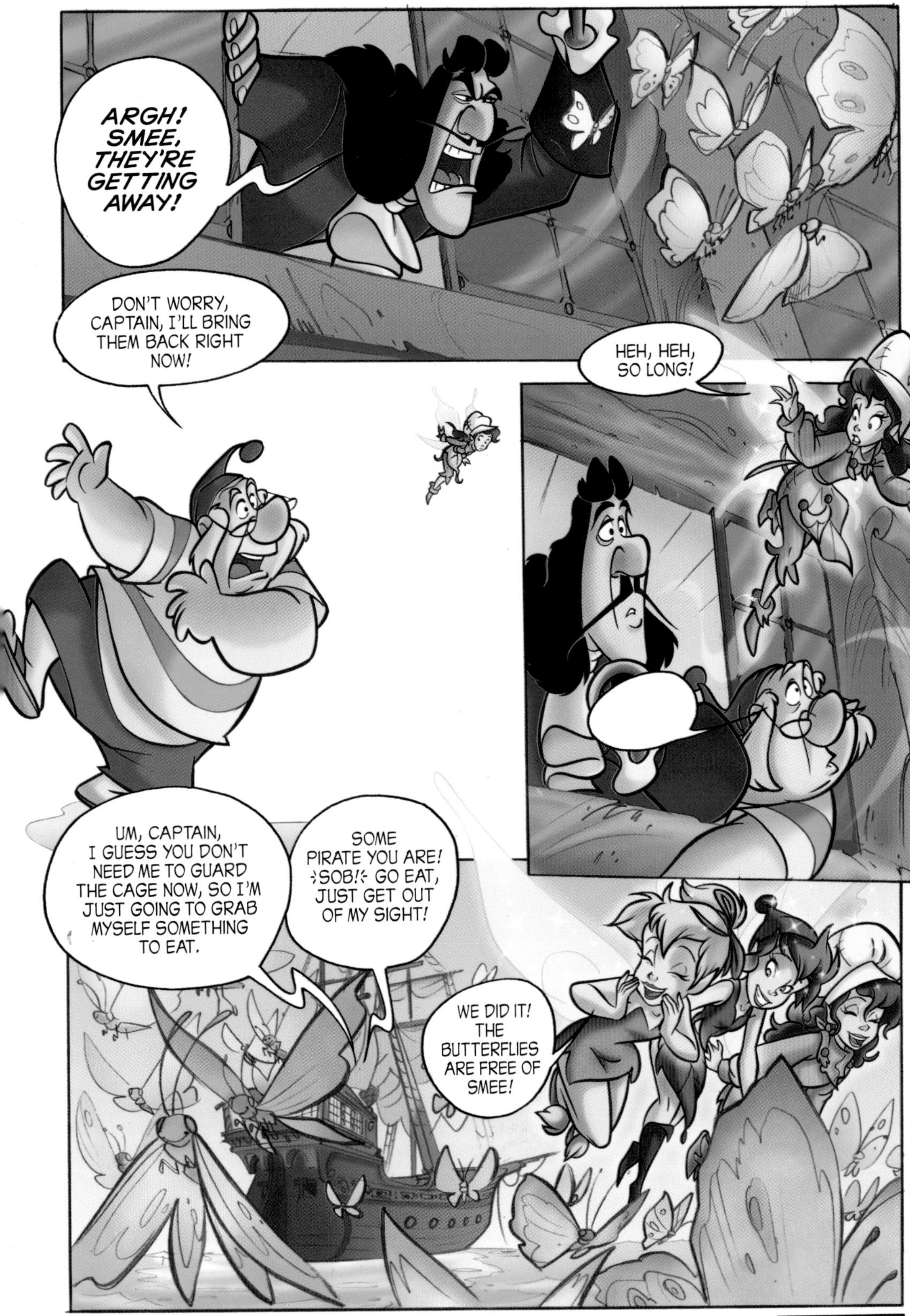
ARGH! SMEE, THEY'RE GETTING AWAY!
DON'T WORRY, CAPTAIN, I'LL BRING THEM BACK RIGHT NOW!
HEH, HEH, SO LONG!
UM, CAPTAIN, I GUESS YOU DON'T NEED ME TO GUARD THE CAGE NOW, SO I'M JUST GOING TO GRAB MYSELF SOMETHING TO EAT.
SOME PIRATE YOU ARE! SOB! GO EAT, JUST GET OUT OF MY SIGHT!
WE DID IT! THE BUTTERFLIES ARE FREE OF SMEE!
THE END

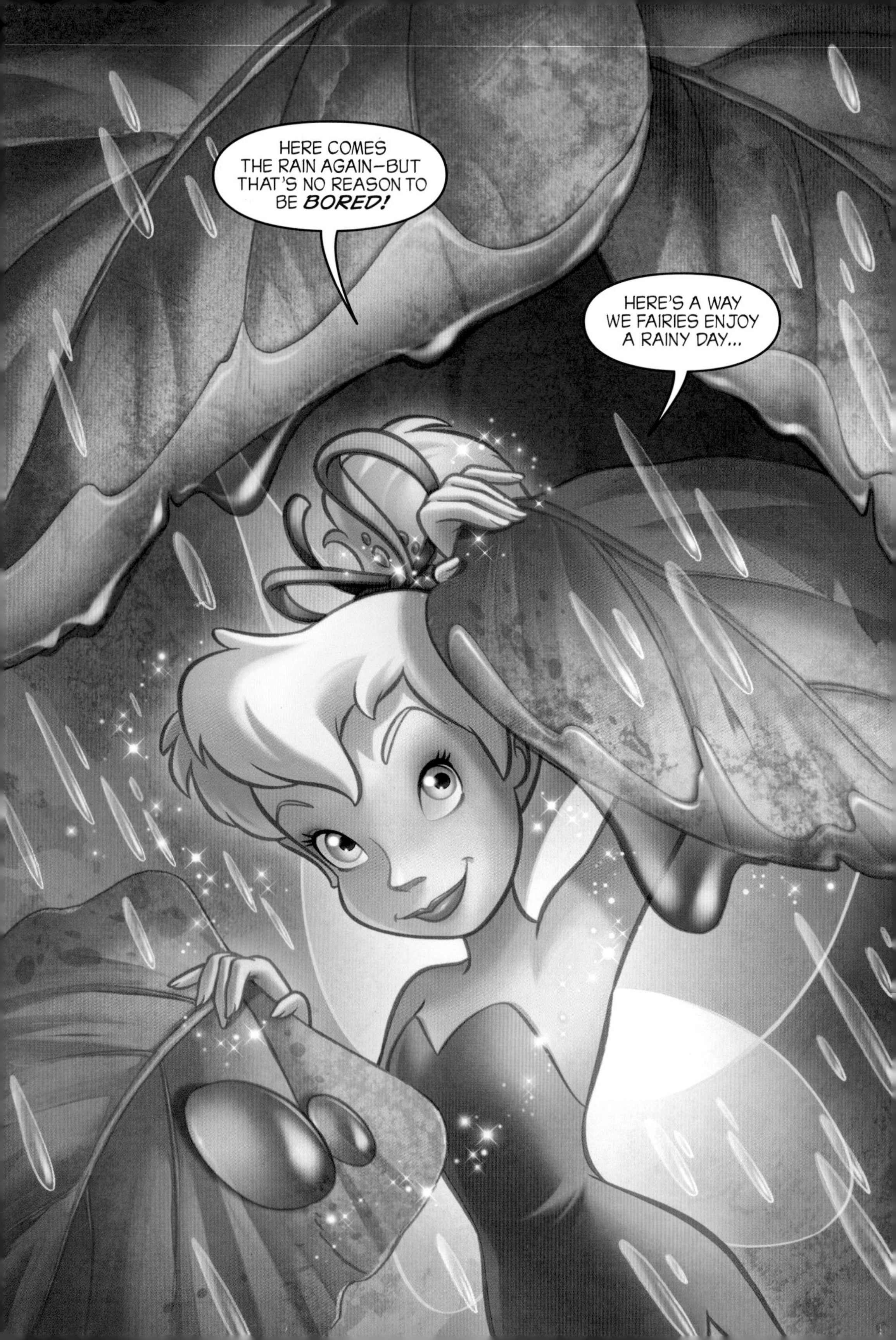
HERE COMES THE RAIN AGAIN—BUT THAT'S NO REASON TO BE **BORED!**
HERE'S A WAY WE FAIRIES ENJOY A RAINY DAY...

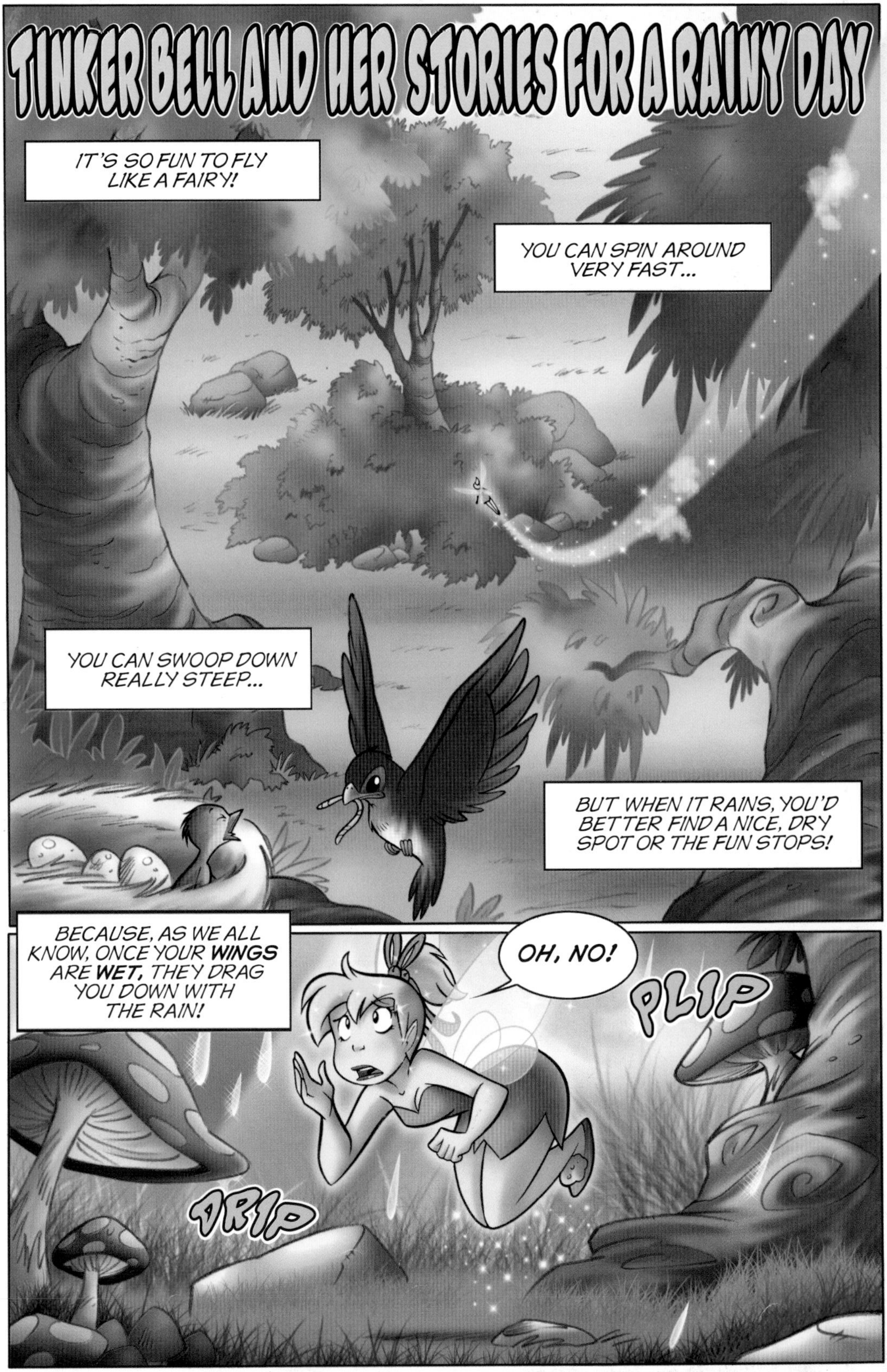
TINKER BELL AND HER STORIES FOR A RAINY DAY
IT'S SO FUN TO FLY LIKE A FAIRY!
YOU CAN SPIN AROUND VERY FAST...
YOU CAN SWOOP DOWN REALLY STEEP...
BUT WHEN IT RAINS, YOU'D BETTER FIND A NICE, DRY SPOT OR THE FUN STOPS!
BECAUSE, AS WE ALL KNOW, ONCE YOUR WINGS ARE WET, THEY DRAG YOU DOWN WITH THE RAIN!
OH, NO!
PLIP
DRIP

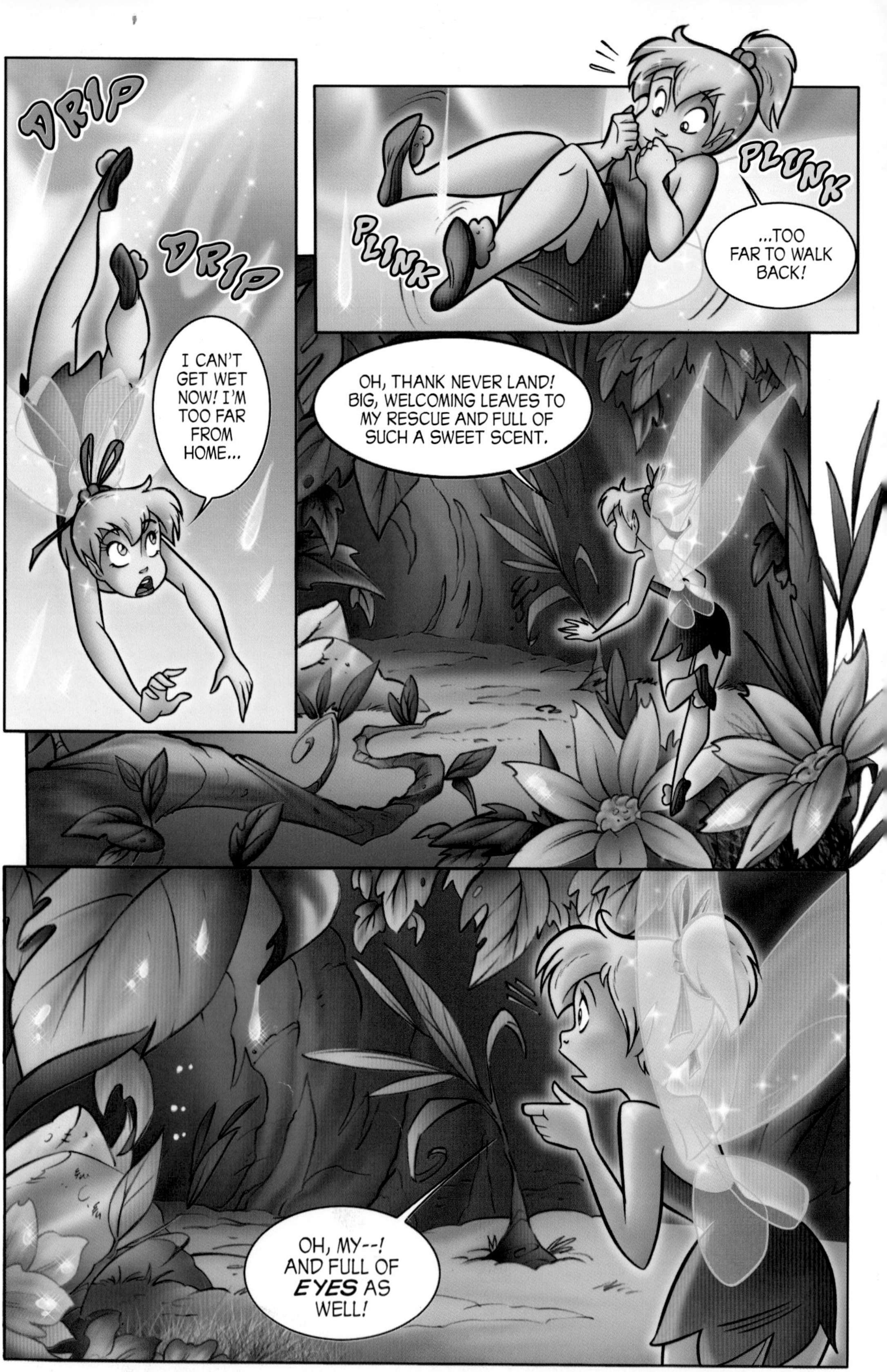
DRIP
DRIP
I CAN'T GET WET NOW! I'M TOO FAR FROM HOME...
PLINK
PLUNK
...TOO FAR TO WALK BACK!
OH, THANK NEVER LAND! BIG, WELCOMING LEAVES TO MY RESCUE AND FULL OF SUCH A SWEET SCENT.
OH, MY--! AND FULL OF EYES AS WELL!

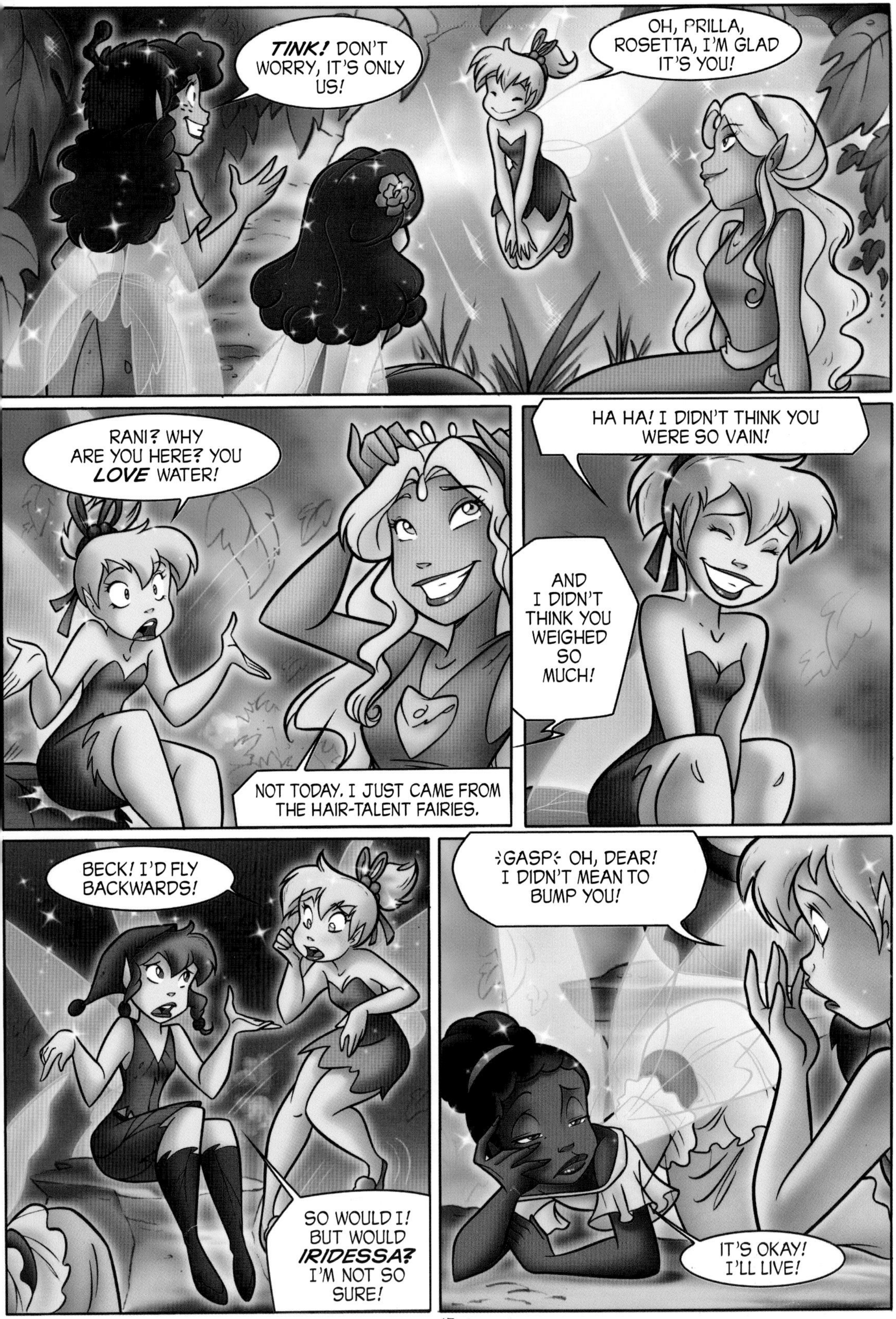
TINK! DON'T WORRY, IT'S ONLY US!
OH, PRILLA, ROSETTA, I'M GLAD IT'S YOU!
RANI? WHY ARE YOU HERE? YOU LOVE WATER!
NOT TODAY. I JUST CAME FROM THE HAIR-TALENT FAIRIES.
HA HA! I DIDN'T THINK YOU WERE SO VAIN!
AND I DIDN'T THINK YOU WEIGHED SO MUCH!
BECK! I'D FLY BACKWARDS!
SO WOULD I! BUT WOULD IRIDESSA? I'M NOT SO SURE!
÷GASP÷ OH, DEAR! I DIDN'T MEAN TO BUMP YOU!
IT'S OKAY! I'LL LIVE!

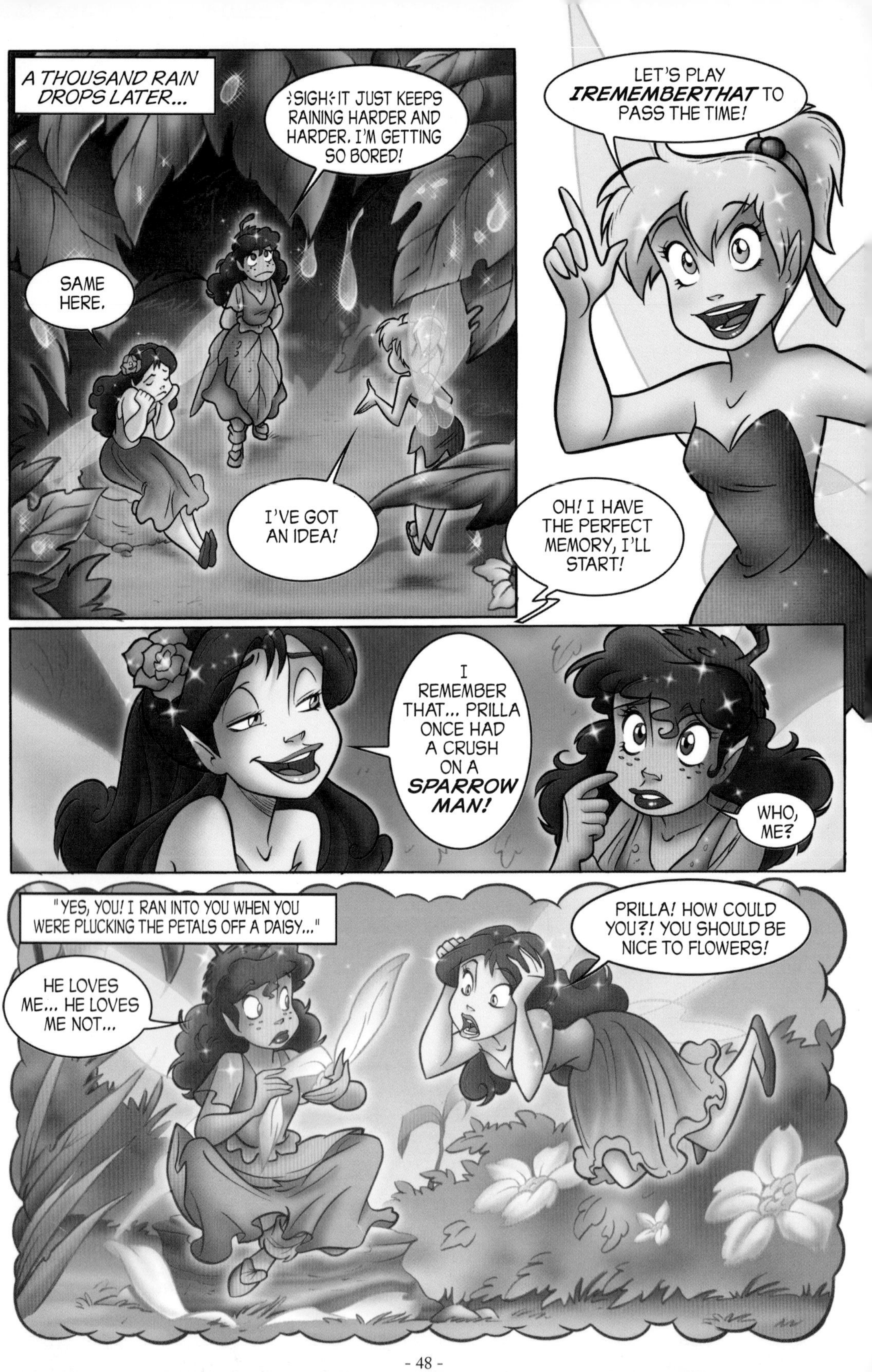
A THOUSAND RAIN DROPS LATER...
⸗SIGH⸗ IT JUST KEEPS RAINING HARDER AND HARDER. I'M GETTING SO BORED!
SAME HERE.
I'VE GOT AN IDEA!
LET'S PLAY IREMEMBERTHAT TO PASS THE TIME!
OH! I HAVE THE PERFECT MEMORY, I'LL START!
I REMEMBER THAT... PRILLA ONCE HAD A CRUSH ON A SPARROW MAN!
WHO, ME?
"YES, YOU! I RAN INTO YOU WHEN YOU WERE PLUCKING THE PETALS OFF A DAISY..."
HE LOVES ME... HE LOVES ME NOT...
PRILLA! HOW COULD YOU?! YOU SHOULD BE NICE TO FLOWERS!

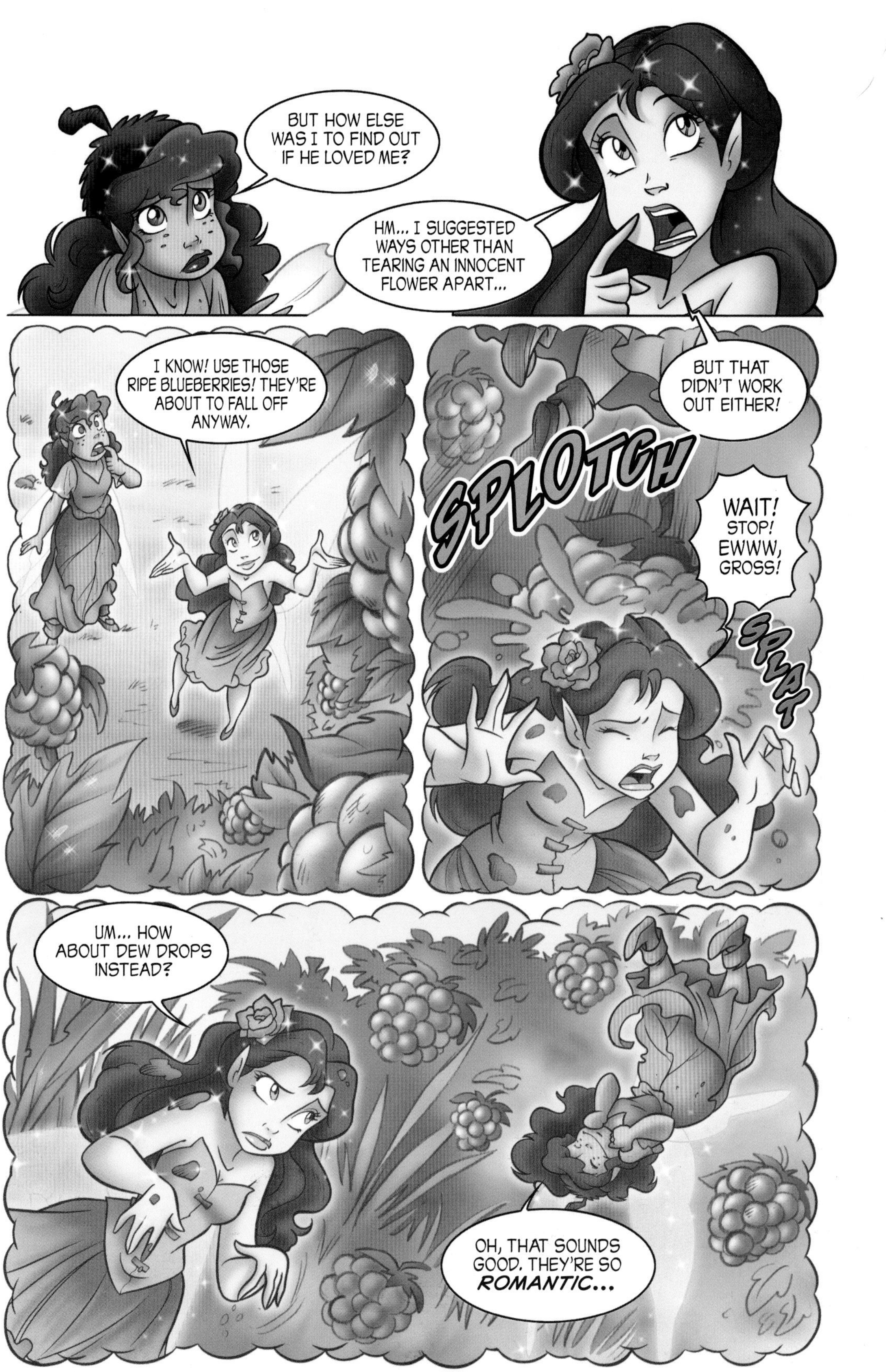
BUT HOW ELSE WAS I TO FIND OUT IF HE LOVED ME?
HM... I SUGGESTED WAYS OTHER THAN TEARING AN INNOCENT FLOWER APART...
I KNOW! USE THOSE RIPE BLUEBERRIES! THEY'RE ABOUT TO FALL OFF ANYWAY.
BUT THAT DIDN'T WORK OUT EITHER!
SPLOTCH
WAIT! STOP! EWWW, GROSS!
SPLAK
UM... HOW ABOUT DEW DROPS INSTEAD?
OH, THAT SOUNDS GOOD. THEY'RE SO ***ROMANTIC...***

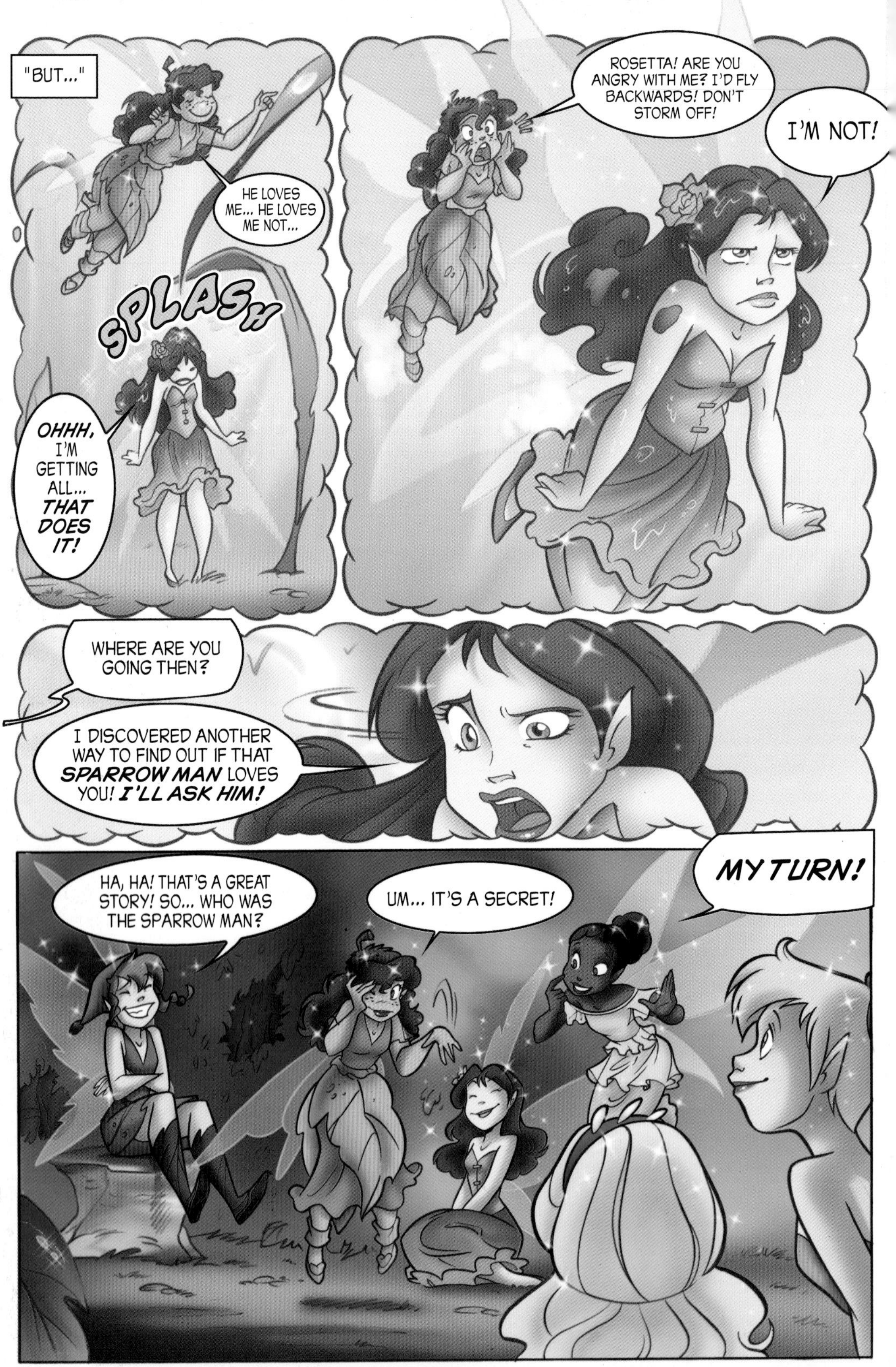
"BUT..."
HE LOVES ME... HE LOVES ME NOT...
SPLASH
OHHH, I'M GETTING ALL... THAT DOES IT!
ROSETTA! ARE YOU ANGRY WITH ME? I'D FLY BACKWARDS! DON'T STORM OFF!
I'M NOT!
WHERE ARE YOU GOING THEN?
I DISCOVERED ANOTHER WAY TO FIND OUT IF THAT SPARROW MAN LOVES YOU! I'LL ASK HIM!
HA, HA! THAT'S A GREAT STORY! SO... WHO WAS THE SPARROW MAN?
UM... IT'S A SECRET!
MY TURN!

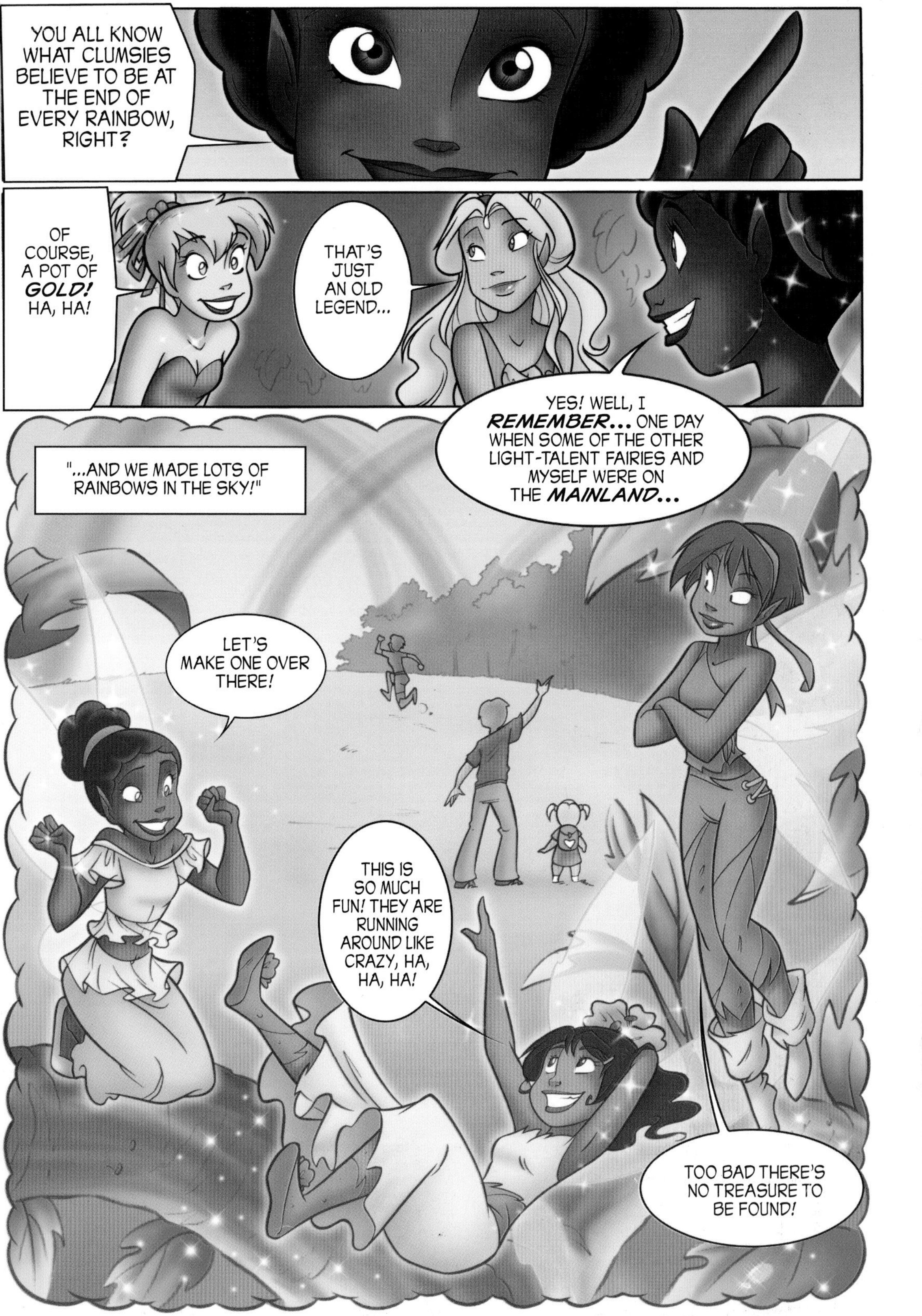
YOU ALL KNOW WHAT CLUMSIES BELIEVE TO BE AT THE END OF EVERY RAINBOW, RIGHT?
OF COURSE, A POT OF GOLD! HA, HA!
THAT'S JUST AN OLD LEGEND...
YES! WELL, I REMEMBER... ONE DAY WHEN SOME OF THE OTHER LIGHT-TALENT FAIRIES AND MYSELF WERE ON THE MAINLAND...
"...AND WE MADE LOTS OF RAINBOWS IN THE SKY!"
LET'S MAKE ONE OVER THERE!
THIS IS SO MUCH FUN! THEY ARE RUNNING AROUND LIKE CRAZY, HA, HA, HA!
TOO BAD THERE'S NO TREASURE TO BE FOUND!

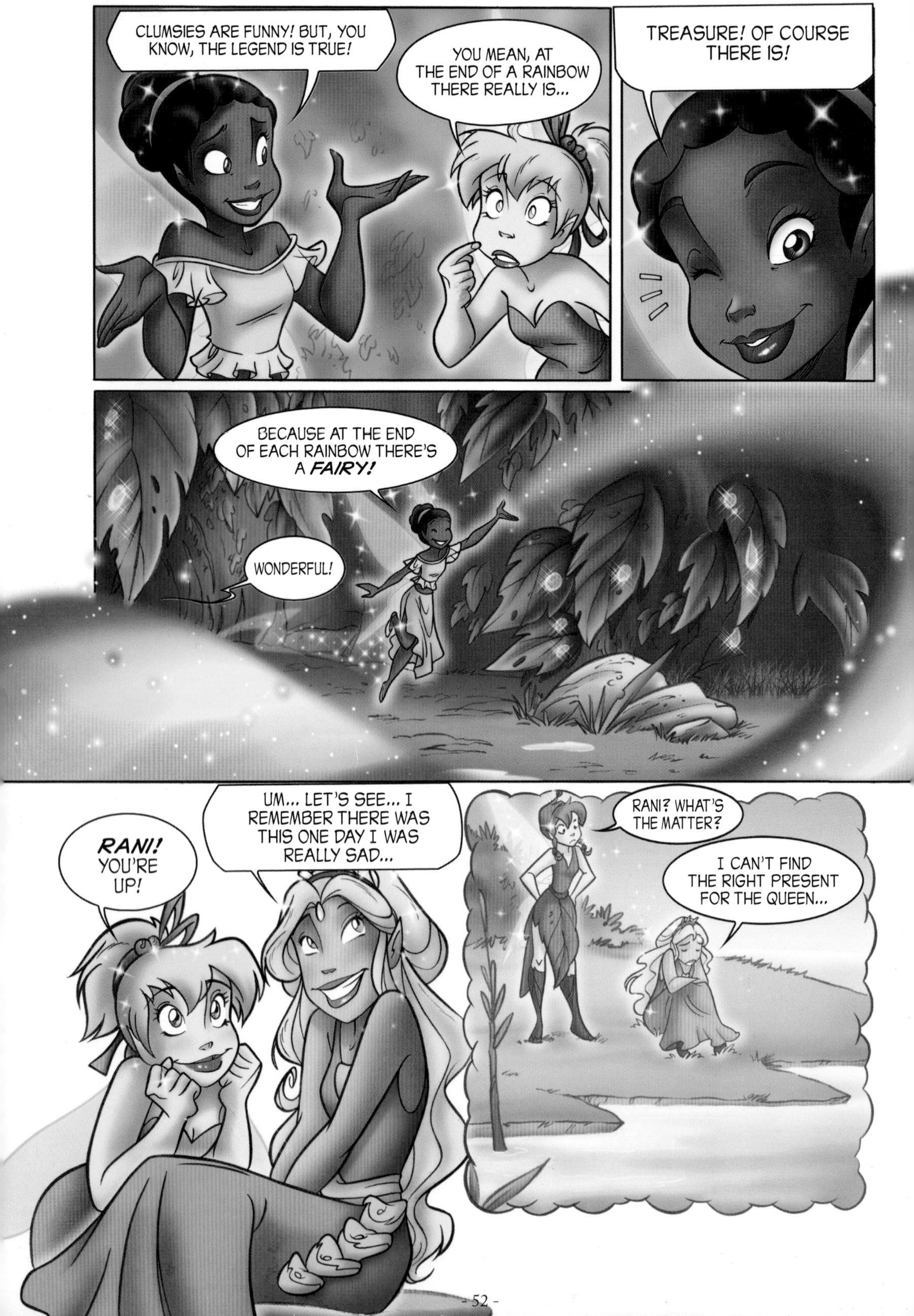
CLUMSIES ARE FUNNY! BUT, YOU KNOW, THE LEGEND IS TRUE!
YOU MEAN, AT THE END OF A RAINBOW THERE REALLY IS...
TREASURE! OF COURSE THERE IS!
BECAUSE AT THE END OF EACH RAINBOW THERE'S A ***FAIRY!***
WONDERFUL!
RANI! YOU'RE UP!
UM... LET'S SEE... I REMEMBER THERE WAS THIS ONE DAY I WAS REALLY SAD...
RANI? WHAT'S THE MATTER?
I CAN'T FIND THE RIGHT PRESENT FOR THE QUEEN...

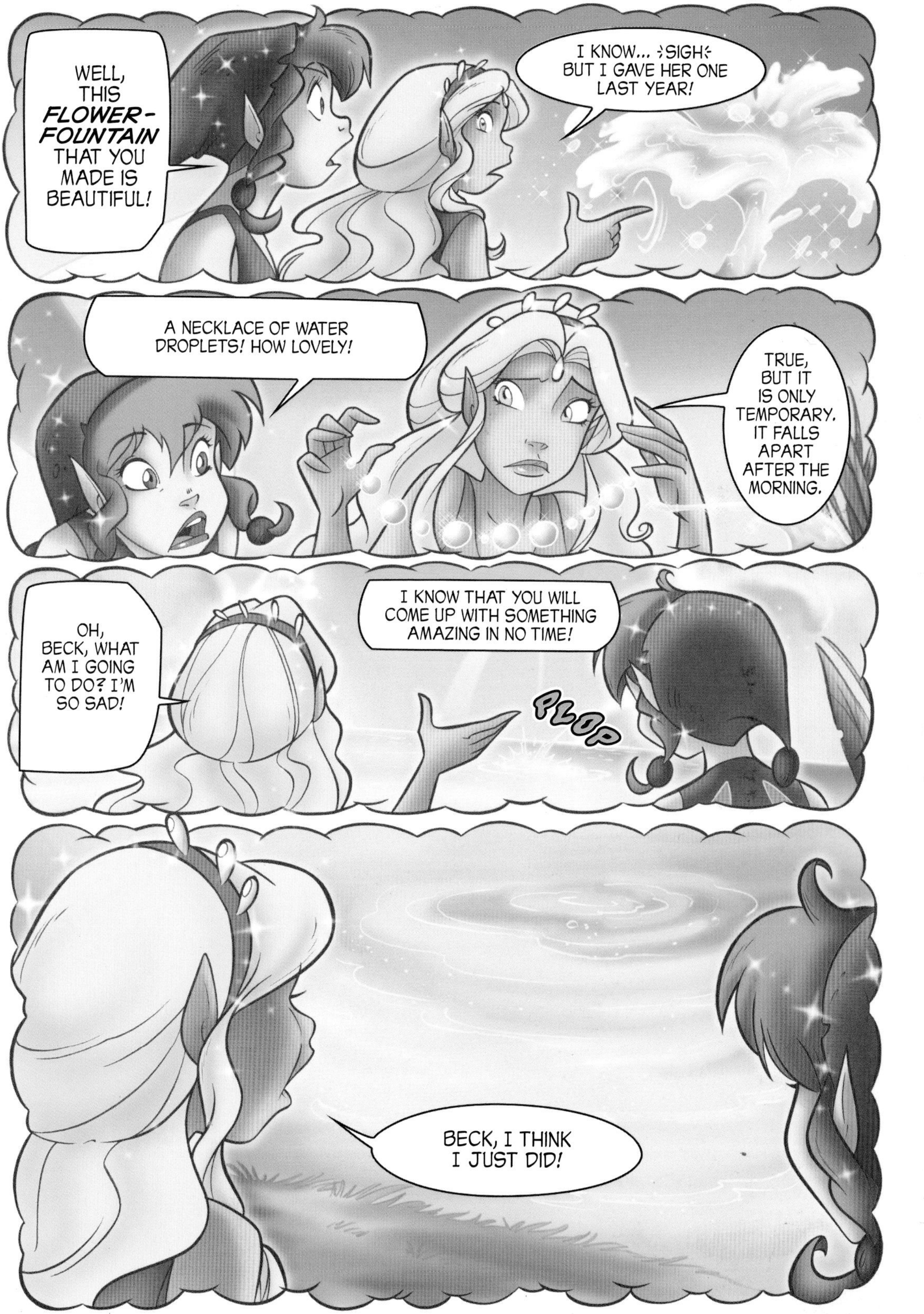

WELL, THIS **FLOWER-FOUNTAIN** THAT YOU MADE IS BEAUTIFUL!
I KNOW... ⁏SIGH⁏ BUT I GAVE HER ONE LAST YEAR!
A NECKLACE OF WATER DROPLETS! HOW LOVELY!
TRUE, BUT IT IS ONLY TEMPORARY. IT FALLS APART AFTER THE MORNING.
OH, BECK, WHAT AM I GOING TO DO? I'M SO SAD!
I KNOW THAT YOU WILL COME UP WITH SOMETHING AMAZING IN NO TIME!
PLOP
BECK, I THINK I JUST DID!

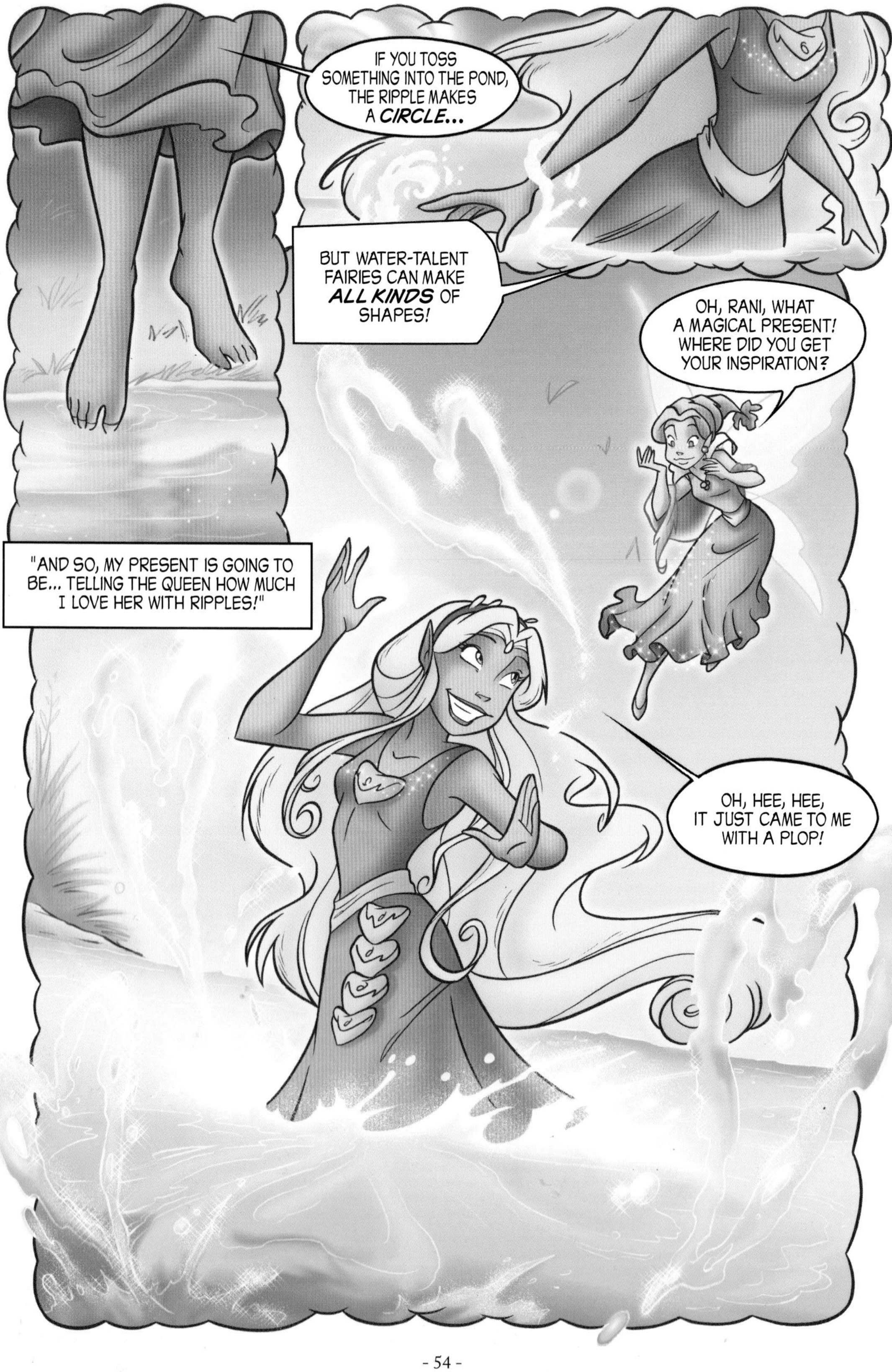
IF YOU TOSS SOMETHING INTO THE POND, THE RIPPLE MAKES A CIRCLE...
BUT WATER-TALENT FAIRIES CAN MAKE ALL KINDS OF SHAPES!
OH, RANI, WHAT A MAGICAL PRESENT! WHERE DID YOU GET YOUR INSPIRATION?
"AND SO, MY PRESENT IS GOING TO BE... TELLING THE QUEEN HOW MUCH I LOVE HER WITH RIPPLES!"
OH, HEE, HEE, IT JUST CAME TO ME WITH A PLOP!

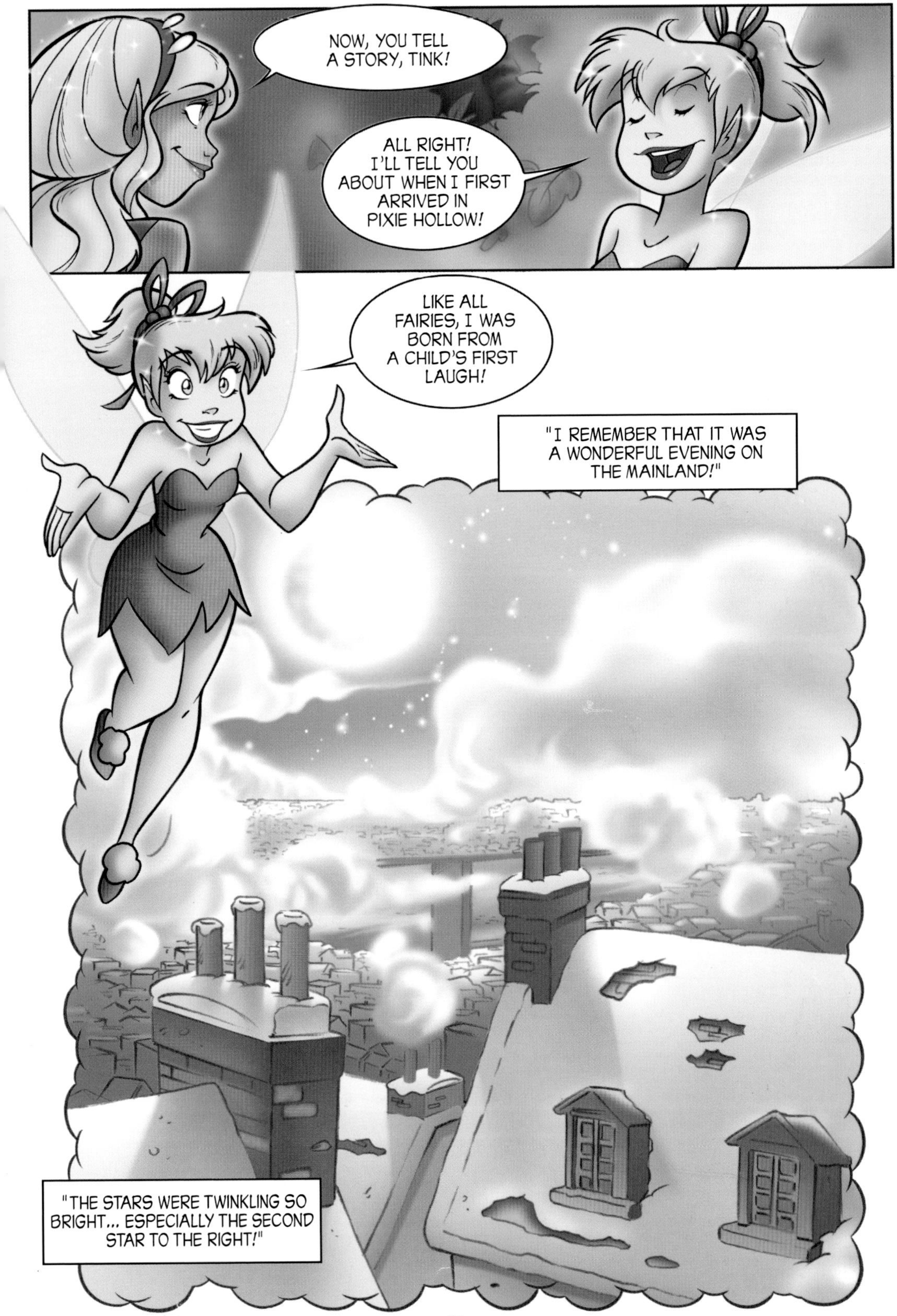
NOW, YOU TELL A STORY, TINK!
ALL RIGHT! I'LL TELL YOU ABOUT WHEN I FIRST ARRIVED IN PIXIE HOLLOW!
LIKE ALL FAIRIES, I WAS BORN FROM A CHILD'S FIRST LAUGH!
"I REMEMBER THAT IT WAS A WONDERFUL EVENING ON THE MAINLAND!"
"THE STARS WERE TWINKLING SO BRIGHT... ESPECIALLY THE SECOND STAR TO THE RIGHT!"

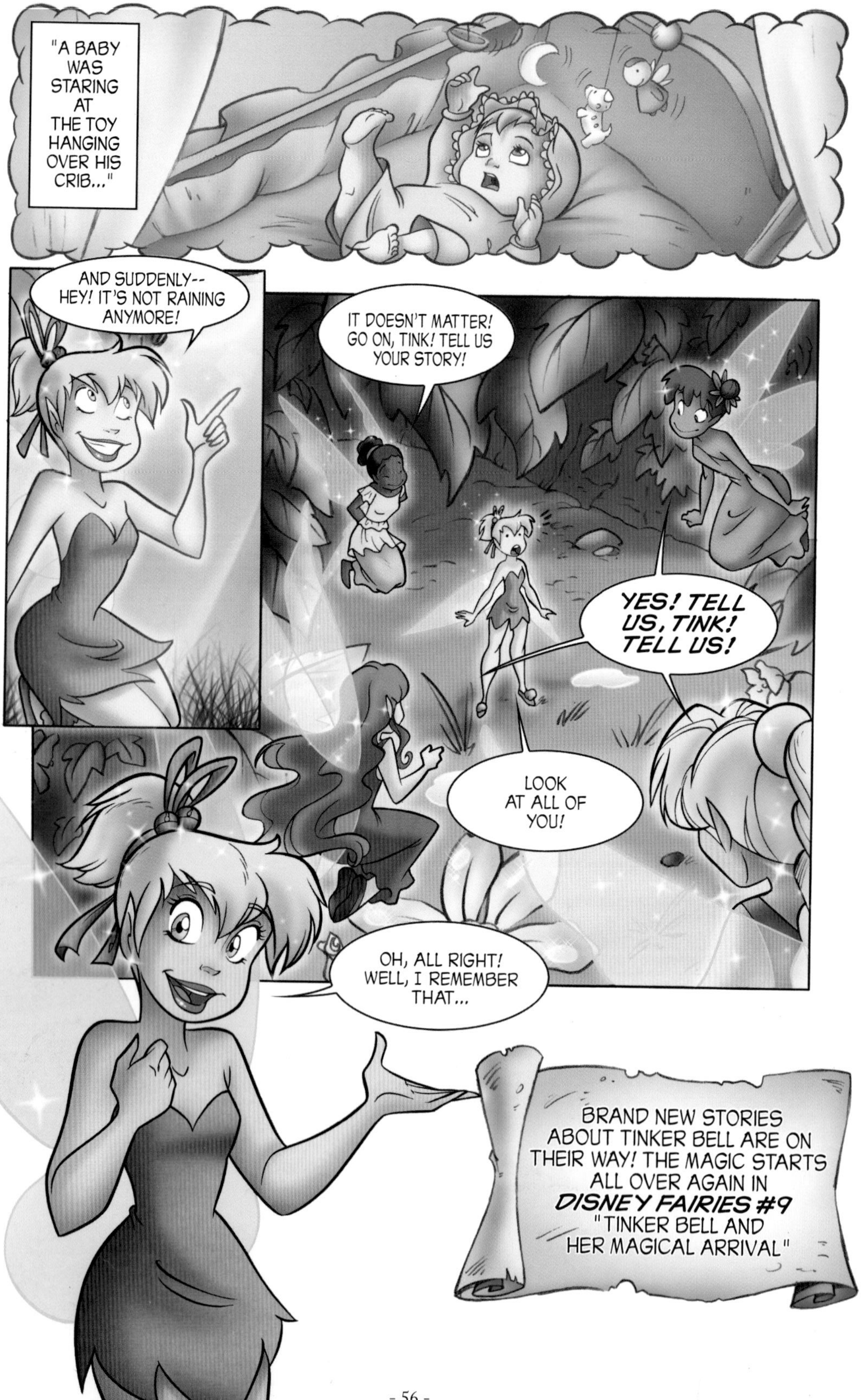
"A BABY WAS STARING AT THE TOY HANGING OVER HIS CRIB..."
AND SUDDENLY-- HEY! IT'S NOT RAINING ANYMORE!
IT DOESN'T MATTER! GO ON, TINK! TELL US YOUR STORY!
YES! TELL US, TINK! TELL US!
LOOK AT ALL OF YOU!
OH, ALL RIGHT! WELL, I REMEMBER THAT...
BRAND NEW STORIES ABOUT TINKER BELL ARE ON THEIR WAY! THE MAGIC STARTS ALL OVER AGAIN IN
DISNEY FAIRIES #9
"TINKER BELL AND HER MAGICAL ARRIVAL"

WATCH OUT FOR
PAPERCUTZ ™

Welcome to the eighth (collect 'em all!) enchanting DISNEY FAIRIES graphic novel from Papercutz, the folks dedicated to creating great graphic novels for all ages. I'm Jim Salicrup, your pixilated Editor-in-Chief, and one-time guest on the Mickey Mouse Club!

While we're relatively certain most of you are well aware of exactly who Tinker Bell and her fellow fairies are, we're not too sure you're fully aware of who and what Papercutz is. Well, fear not, I'm more than happy to shed a little light on that mystery. It all started in 2005, when Papercutz publisher Terry Nantier and I got together to start a new comics publishing company that would produce material for all ages. After all, both Terry and I have loved comics since we were kids, and it seemed that there was too few comics being published back then that were suitable for all ages. The reason for that is really strange. In a nutshell, comics were being created and produced by adults and sold and distributed to comicbook stores run by adults and sold to their primarily adult customers. While that's all well and good if you're an adult, we wondered about where the next generation of comics fans would come if nothing was being produced for younger fans?

Furthermore, there was very little being produced for female comics fans. Again, the reason was strange—very few females would shop in comicbook stores, so very few comics were produced for female audiences. It was a crazy situation! But everything changed when regular bookstores started giving shelf space to graphic novels and Manga. Finally the comics and their intended audience (that's you!) we're starting to come together. So, while overall that's a wonderful thing, it too has its limitations. For example, if one of our graphic novels is located in the "childrens section" some older folks may assume the graphic novel is too juvenile for them. As you can see, there is no simple solution yet, but at least we're making progress. More and more comicbook stores are realizing what a wonderful idea it is to carry such graphic novels as DISNEY FAIRIES, GERONIMO STILTON, and THE SMURFS (Not to mention DANCE CLASS, ERNEST & REBECCA, GARFIELD & Co, and NINJAGO) and we're very thankful for that!

There is a little something you can do to help. It's not that difficult. All you need to do, if you're interested in any of those Papercutz graphic novels just mentioned, is to ask your friendly comicbook store worker or bookstore employee to order the books you're interested in. Chances are they'll be happy to do that for you, and it'll help convince them that there are lots of people out there who are looking for this type of material. Of course, if you're favorite comicbook shop or bookstore already carries plenty of Papercutz graphic novels, then it certainly won't hurt to let them know how thankful you are that they do.

It's been several years since Papercutz started, and the good news is that there seems to be more and more comics and graphic novels being created for all ages. Partly that's thanks to you—for supporting titles such as DISNEY FAIRIES. And on behalf of everyone at Papercutz, we're very thankful to you for your continued support!

So, until we meet again in DISNEY FAIRIES #9 " Tinker Bell and Her Magical Arrival," don't forget to keep believing in "faith, trust, and pixie dust"!

Thanks,

Jim

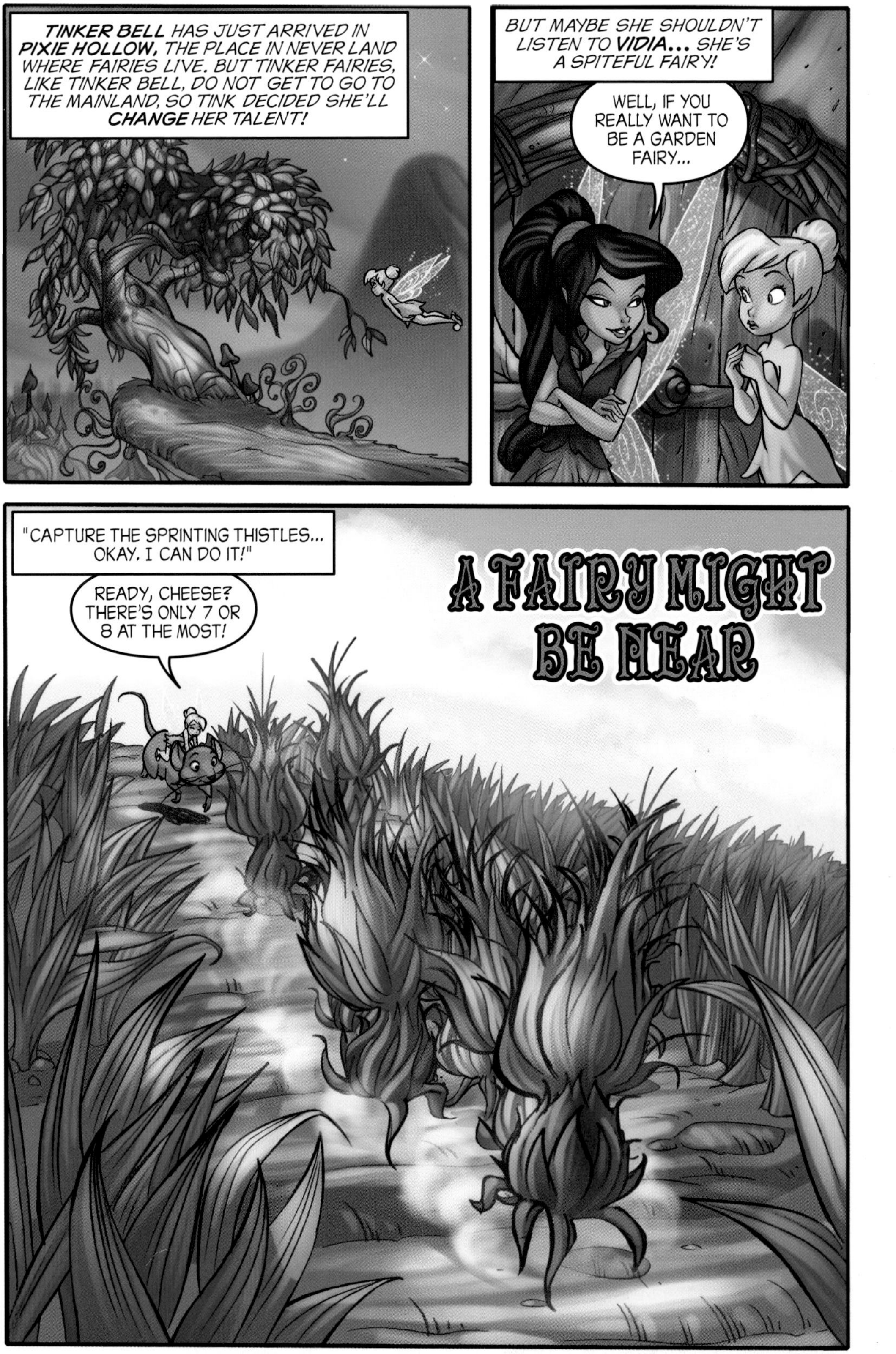
TINKER BELL HAS JUST ARRIVED IN PIXIE HOLLOW, THE PLACE IN NEVER LAND WHERE FAIRIES LIVE. BUT TINKER FAIRIES, LIKE TINKER BELL, DO NOT GET TO GO TO THE MAINLAND, SO TINK DECIDED SHE'LL CHANGE HER TALENT!
BUT MAYBE SHE SHOULDN'T LISTEN TO VIDIA... SHE'S A SPITEFUL FAIRY!
WELL, IF YOU REALLY WANT TO BE A GARDEN FAIRY...
"CAPTURE THE SPRINTING THISTLES... OKAY. I CAN DO IT!"
READY, CHEESE? THERE'S ONLY 7 OR 8 AT THE MOST!
A FAIRY MIGHT BE NEAR

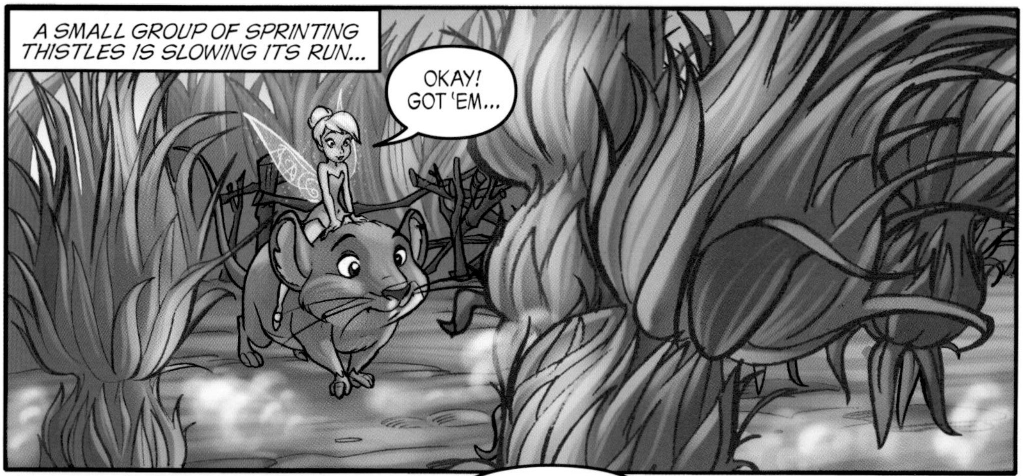
A SMALL GROUP OF SPRINTING THISTLES IS SLOWING ITS RUN...
OKAY! GOT 'EM...

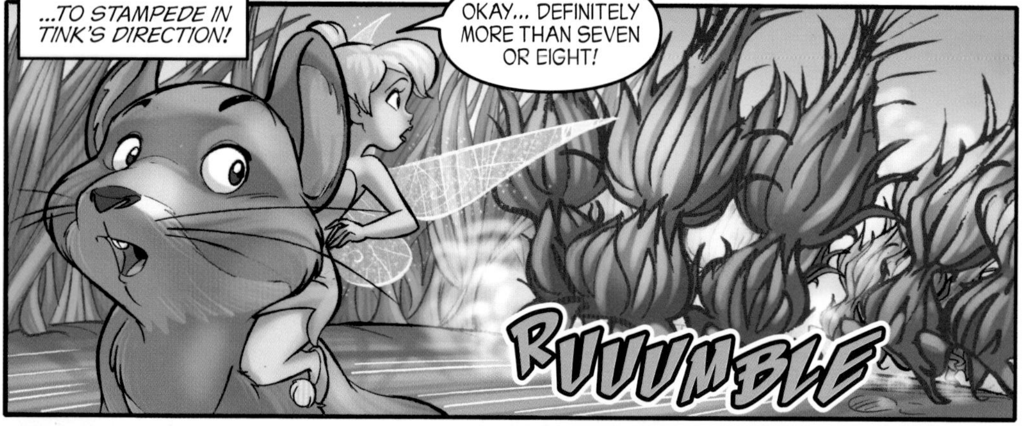
...TO STAMPEDE IN TINK'S DIRECTION!
OKAY... DEFINITELY MORE THAN SEVEN OR EIGHT!
RUUUMBLE

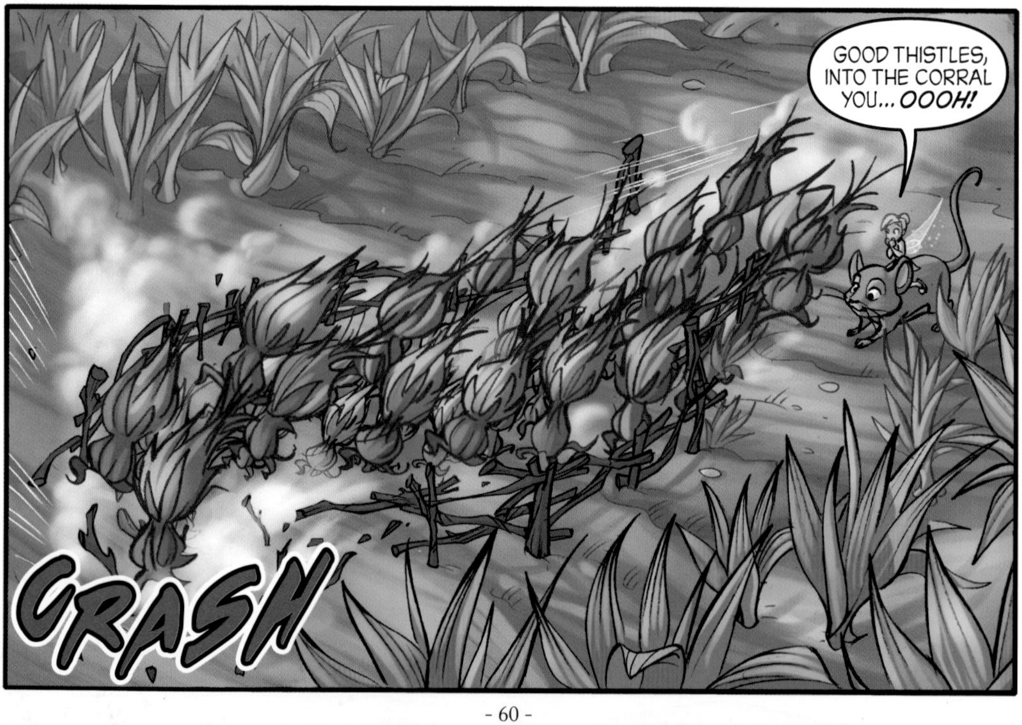
GOOD THISTLES, INTO THE CORRAL YOU... OOOH!
CRASH

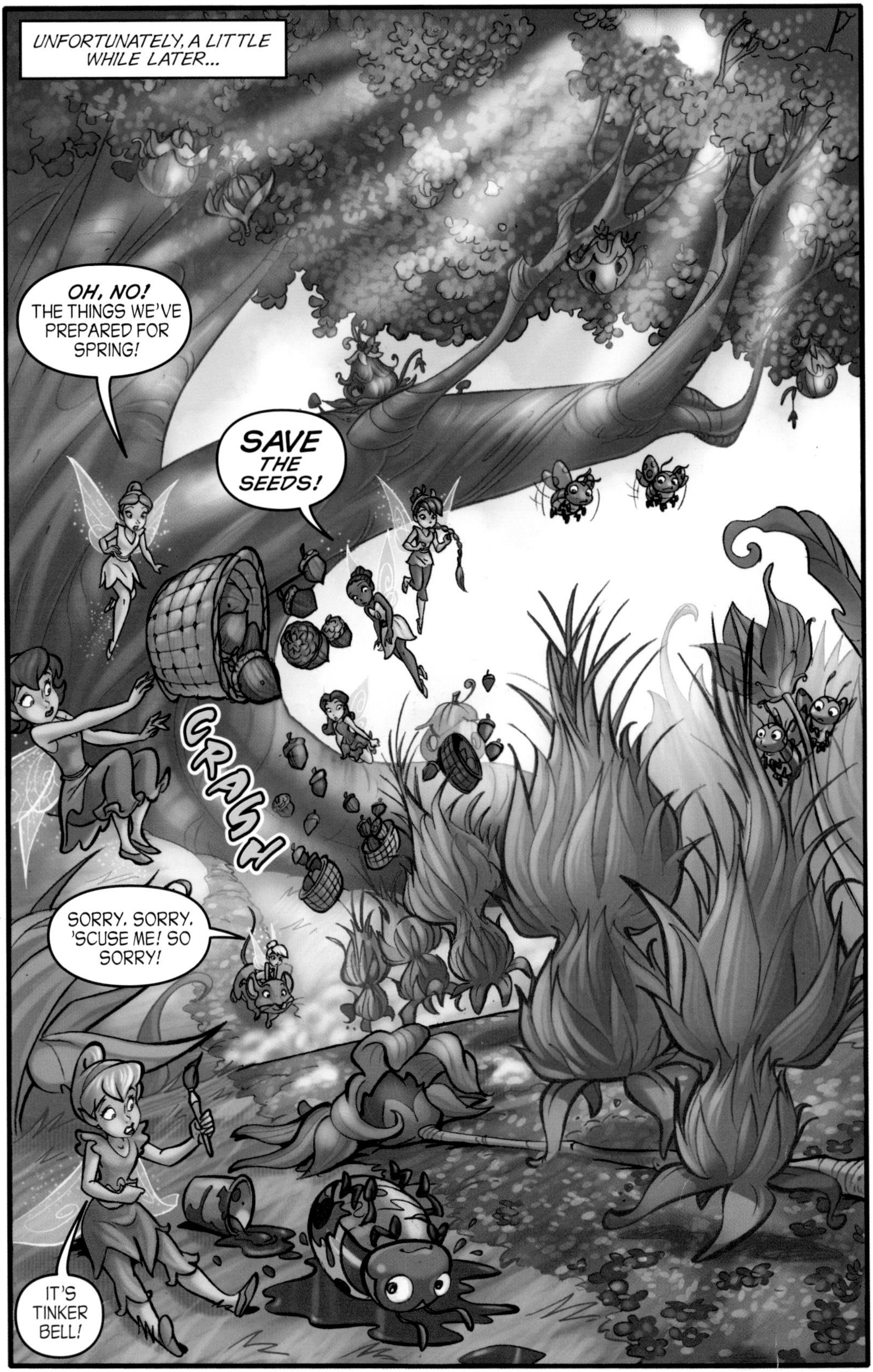
UNFORTUNATELY, A LITTLE WHILE LATER...
OH, NO! THE THINGS WE'VE PREPARED FOR SPRING!
SAVE THE SEEDS!
CRASH
SORRY. SORRY. 'SCUSE ME! SO SORRY!
IT'S TINKER BELL!

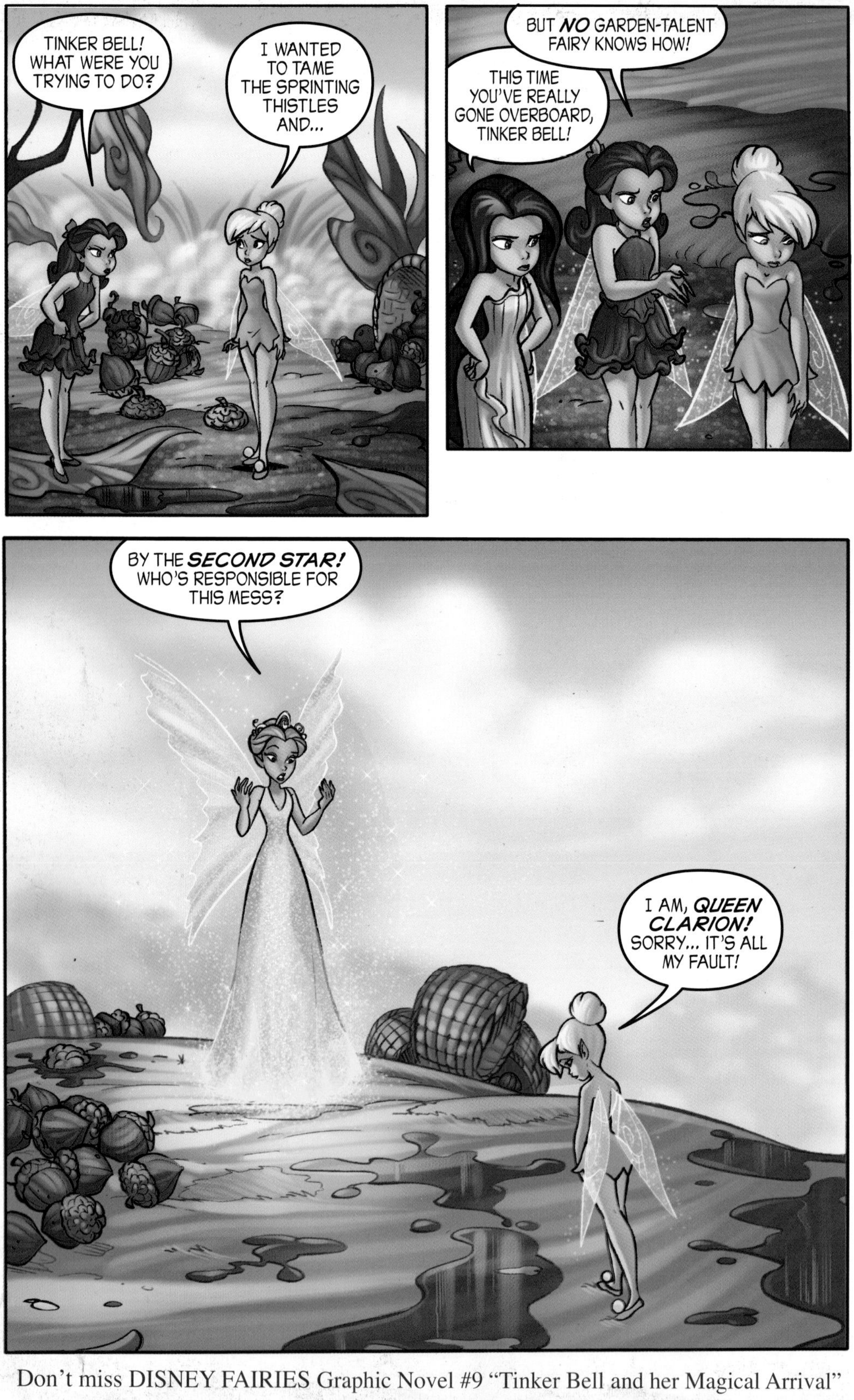
TINKER BELL! WHAT WERE YOU TRYING TO DO?
I WANTED TO TAME THE SPRINTING THISTLES AND...
BUT NO GARDEN-TALENT FAIRY KNOWS HOW!
THIS TIME YOU'VE REALLY GONE OVERBOARD, TINKER BELL!
BY THE SECOND STAR! WHO'S RESPONSIBLE FOR THIS MESS?
I AM, QUEEN CLARION! SORRY... IT'S ALL MY FAULT!

Don't miss DISNEY FAIRIES Graphic Novel #9 "Tinker Bell and her Magical Arrival"

THE CALL OF THE WILD

By Jack London

Adapted by Charles Dixon and Ricardo Villagran

PAPERCUTZ

Available Now at Booksellers Everywhere